Leave the
World Behind

ALSO BY RUMAAN ALAM

That Kind of Mother

Rich and Pretty

Leave the World Behind

A Novel

Rumaan Alam

HARPER LARGE PRINT

An Imprint of HarperCollinsPublishers

"Angela"
Written by Bill Callahan
Published by Rough Trade Publishing
By arrangement with Bank Robber Music

HarperCollins books may be purchased for educational, business, or sales promotional use. For information, please e-mail the Special Markets Department at SPsales@harpercollins.com.

FIRST HARPER LARGE PRINT EDITION

ISBN: 978-0-06-302922-4

Library of Congress Cataloging-in-Publication Data is available upon request.

21 22 23 24 LSC 10 9 8 7 6 5 4 3

for Simon and for Xavier

Love goes on like birdsong,
As soon as possible after a bomb.
—Bill Callahan, "Angela"

1

Well, the sun was shining. They felt that boded well—people turn any old thing into an omen. It was all just to say no clouds were to be seen. The sun where the sun always was. The sun persistent and indifferent.

Roads merged into one another. The traffic congealed. Their gray car was a bell jar, a microclimate: air-conditioning, the funk of adolescence (sweat, feet, sebum), Amanda's French shampoo, the rustle of debris, for there always was that. The car was Clay's domain, and he was lax enough that it accrued the talus of oats from granola bars bought in bulk, the unexplained tube sock, a subscription insert from the *New Yorker*, a twisted tissue, ossified with snot, that wisp of white plastic peeled from the back of a Band-Aid who knew when. Kids were always needing a Band-Aid, pink skin splitting like summer fruit.

The sunlight on their arms was reassuring. The windows were tinted with a protectant to keep cancer at bay. There was news of an intensifying hurricane season, storms with fanciful names from a preapproved list. Amanda turned down the radio. Was it sexist, somehow, that Clay drove, and always did? Well: Amanda had no patience for the attendant sacraments of alternate-side-of-the-street parking and the twelve-thousand-mile checkup. Besides, Clay took pride in that kind of thing. He was a professor, and that seemed to correlate with his relish for life's useful tasks: bundling old newspapers for recycling, scattering chemical pellets on the sidewalk when the weather turned icy, replacing lightbulbs, unclogging stopped sinks with a miniature plunger.

The car was not so new as to be luxurious nor so old as to be bohemian. A middle-class thing for middle-class people, engineered not to offend more than to appeal, purchased at a showroom with mirrored walls, some half-hearted balloons, and several more salesmen than customers, lingering in twos or threes, jingling the change in the pockets of their Men's Wearhouse slacks. Sometimes, in the parking lot, Clay would approach some other iteration of the car (it was a popular model, "graphite"), frustrated when the keyless entry system failed to engage.

Archie was sixteen. He wore misshapen sneakers the size of bread loaves. There was a scent of milk about him, as there was to young babies, and beneath that, sweat and hormone. To mitigate all this Archie sprayed a chemical into the thatch under his arms, a smell unlike any in nature, a focus group's consensus of the masculine ideal. Rose paid better attention. The shadow of a young girl in flower; a bloodhound might find the metal beneath the whiff of entry-level cosmetics, the pubescent predilection for fake apples and cherries. They smelled, everyone did, but you couldn't drive the expressway with the windows open, it was too loud. "I have to take this." Amanda held the telephone aloft, warning them, even though no one was saying anything. Archie looked at his own phone, Rose at hers, both with games and parentally preapproved social media. Archie was texting with his friend Dillon, whose two dads were atoning for their ongoing divorce by letting him spend the summer smoking pot in the uppermost floor of their Bergen Street brownstone. Rose had already posted multiple photographs of the trip, though they'd only just crossed the county line.

"Hey Jocelyn—" That telephones knew who was calling obviated nicety. Amanda was account director,

Jocelyn account supervisor and one of her three direct reports in the parlance of the modern office. Jocelyn, of Korean parentage, had been born in South Carolina, and Amanda continued to feel that the woman's mealymouthed accent was incongruous. This was so racist she could never admit it to anyone.

"I'm so sorry to bother you—" Jocelyn's syncopated breath. It was less that Amanda was fearsome than that power was. Amanda had started her career in the studio of a temperamental Dane with a haircut like a tonsure. She'd run into the man at a restaurant the previous winter and felt queasy.

"It's not a problem." Amanda wasn't magnanimous. The call was a relief. She wanted her colleagues to need her as God wants people to keep praying.

Clay drummed fingers on the leather steering wheel, earning a sideways glance from his wife. He looked at the mirror to confirm that his children were still there, a habit forged in their infancy. The rhythm of their breath was steady. The phones worked on them like those bulbous flutes did on cobras.

None of them really saw the highway landscape. The brain abets the eye; eventually your expectations of a thing supersede the thing itself. Yellow-and-black pictographs, hillocks fading into prefab concrete walls, the occasional glimpse of split-level, railroad crossing, baseball diamond, aboveground pool. Amanda nodded when she took calls, not for the benefit of the person on the other end of the phone but to prove to herself that she was engaged. Sometimes, amid the head nodding, she forgot to listen.

"Jocelyn—" Amanda tried to find some wisdom. Jocelyn didn't need Amanda's input as much as she did her consent. Office hierarchy was arbitrary, like everything. "That's fine. I think that's wise. We're just on the expressway. You can call, don't worry about it. But service is spotty once we get farther out. I had this problem last summer, you remember?" She paused, and was embarrassed; why would her underling remember Amanda's previous year's vacation plans? "We're going farther out this year!" She made it into a joke. "But call, or email, of course, it's fine. Good luck."

"Everything's okay back at the office?" Clay could never resist pronouncing "the office" with a twist of something. It was synecdoche for her profession, which he largely—but not entirely—understood. A spouse should have her own life, and Amanda's was quite apart from his. Maybe that helped explain their happiness. At least half of the couples they knew were divorced.

"It's fine." One of her most reached-for truisms was that some percentage of jobs were indistinguishable from one another, as they all involved the sending of emails assessing the job itself. A workday was several communiqués about the workday then under way, some bureaucratic politesse, seventy minutes at lunch, twenty minutes caroming around the open-plan, twenty-five minutes drinking coffee. Sometimes her part in the charade felt silly and other times it felt urgent.

The traffic was not so bad, and then, as highways narrowed into streets, it was. Akin to the final, arduous leg of a salmon's trip back home, only with lush green medians and mini malls of rain-stained stucco. The towns were either blue collar and full of Central Americans or prosperous and populated by the white demimonde of plumbers and interior designers and real estate brokers. The actual rich lived in some other realm, like Narnia. You had to happen onto it, trace speedbumpy roads to their inevitable terminus, a cul-de-sac, a shingled mansion, a view of a pond. The air was that sweet cocktail of ocean breeze and happenstance, good for tomatoes and corn, but you thought you could also catch a note of luxury cars, fine art, those soft textiles rich people leave piled on their sofas.

"Should we stop for a bite?" Clay yawned at the end of this sentence, a strangled sound.

"I'm starving." Archie's hyperbole.

"Let's go to Burger King!" Rose had spied the restaurant.

Clay could feel his wife tense up. She preferred that
they eat healthily (especially Rose). He could pick up
her disapproval like sonar. It was like the swell that
presaged an erection. They'd been married sixteen
years.

Amanda ate French fries. Archie requested a gro-
tesque number of little briquettes of fried chicken. He
dumped these into a paper bag, mixed in some French
fries, dribbled in the contents of a small foil-topped container of a sweet and sticky brown sauce, and chewed
contentedly.

"Gross." Rose did not approve of her brother, because he was her brother. She ate, less primly than she
thought, a hamburger, mayonnaise ringing her pink
lips. "Mom, Hazel dropped a pin—can you look at this
and see how far her house is?"

Amanda remembered being shocked by how loud
the children had been as infants at her breast. Draining
and suckling like the sound of plumbing, dispassion-
ate burps and muted flatulence like a dud firecracker,
animal and unashamed. She reached behind her for the
girl's phone, greasy from food and fingers, hot from
overuse. "Honey, this is not going to be anywhere near

us." Hazel was less a friend than one of Rose's obsessions. Rose was too young to understand, but Hazel's father was a director at Lazard; the two family's vacations would not much resemble one another.

"Just *look*. You said maybe we could drive over there."

That was the kind of thing she would suggest when half paying attention and come to rue, later, because the kids remembered her promises. Amanda looked at the phone. "It's East Hampton, honey. It's an hour at least. More than, depending on the day."

Rose leaned back in her seat, audibly disgusted. "Can I have my phone back, please?"

Amanda turned and looked at her daughter, frustrated and flushed. "I'm sorry, but I don't want to sit through two hours of summer traffic for a playdate. Not when I'm on vacation."

The girl folded her arms across her chest, a pout like a weapon. Playdate! She was insulted.

Archie chewed at his reflection in the window.

Clay ate as he drove. Amanda would be furious if they were killed in a collision because he'd been distracted by a seven-hundred-calorie sandwich.

The roads narrowed further. Farm stands—honor system: felted green pints of hairy raspberries, moldering in their juices, and a wooden box for your five-dollar bill—on some of the drives wending off the main road. Everything was so green it was frankly a little crazy. You wanted to eat it: get out of the car, get down on all fours, and bite into the earth itself.

"Let's get some air." Clay opened all of the windows, banishing the stink of his farting children. He slowed the car because the road was curvy, seductive, a hip switched back and forth. Designer mailboxes like a hobo sign: good taste and great wealth, pass on by. You couldn't see anything, the trees were that full. Signs warned of deer, idiotic and inured to the presence of humans. They strutted into the streets confidently, walleyed and therefore blind. You saw their corpses everywhere, nut brown and pneumatic with death.

They rounded a bend and confronted a vehicle. Archie at age four, would have known the word for it: *gooseneck trailer*, a huge, empty conveyance being towed by a determined tractor. The driver ignored the car at his back, the local's nonchalance for a familiar invasive species, as the trailer huffed over the road's swells. It was more than a mile before it turned off toward its home homestead, and by that point Ariadne's thread, or whatever bound them to the satellites overhead, had snapped. The GPS had no idea where they were, and they had to follow the directions that Amanda, adept planner, had thought to copy into her notebook. Left then right then left then left then another mile or so, then left again, then two more miles, then right, not quite lost but not quite not lost.

2

The house was brick, painted white. There was something alluring about that red so transformed. The house looked old but new. It looked solid but light. Perhaps that was a fundamentally American desire, or just a modern urge, to want a house, a car, a book, a pair of shoes, to embody these contradictions.

Amanda had found the place on Airbnb. "The Ultimate Escape," the ad proclaimed. She respected the chummy advertising-speak of the description. *Step into our beautiful house and leave the world behind.* She'd handed the laptop, hot enough to incubate tumors in her abdomen, over to Clay. He nodded, said something noncommittal.

But Amanda had insisted upon this vacation. The promotion came with a raise. So soon, Rose would vanish into high school disdain. For this fleeting moment, the children were still mostly children, even if Archie approached six feet tall. Amanda could if not conjure at least remember Archie's high girlish voice, the chunk of Rose against her hip. An old saw, but on your deathbed would you remember the night you took the clients to that old steakhouse on Thirty-Sixth Street and asked after their wives, or bobbing about in the pool with your kids, dark lashes beaded with chlorinated water?

"This looks nice." Clay switched off the car. The kids released seat belts and pushed open doors and leaped onto the gravel, eager as Stasi.

"Don't go far," Amanda said, though this was nonsense. There was nowhere to go. Maybe the woods. She did worry about Lyme disease. This was just her maternal practice, to interject with authority. The children had long since ceased hearing her daily plaints.

The gravel made its gravelly sound under Clay's leather driving shoes. "How do we get in?"

"There's a lockbox." Amanda consulted her phone. There was no service. They weren't even on a road. She held the thing over her head, but the little bars refused to fill. She had saved this information. "The lockbox . . . on the fence by the pool heater. Code six two nine two. The key inside opens the side door."

The house was obscured by a sculpted hedgerow, someone's pride, like a snowbank, like a wall. The front yard was bound by a picket fence, white, not a trace of irony in it. There was another fence, this one wood and wire, around the pool, which made the insurance more affordable, and also the home's owners knew that sometimes deer strayed into attractive nuisances, and if you were away for a couple of weeks, the stupid thing would drown, swell, explode, a horrifying mess. Clay fetched the key. Amanda stood in the astonishing, humid afternoon, listening to that strange sound of almost quiet that she missed, or claimed she missed, because they lived in the city. You could hear the thrum of some insect or frog or maybe it was both, the wind tossing about the leaves, the sense of a plane or a lawn mower or maybe it was traffic on a highway somewhere distant that reached you just as the persistent beat of the ocean did when you were near the ocean. They were not near the ocean. No, they could not afford to be, but they could almost hear it, an act of will, of recompense.

"Here we are." Clay unlocked the door, needlessly narrating. He did that sometimes, and caught himself doing it, chastened. The house had that hush expensive houses do. Silence meant the house was plumb, solid, its organs working in happy harmony. The respiration of the central air-conditioning, the vigilance of the expensive fridge, the reliable intelligence of all those digital displays marking the time in almost-synchronicity. At a preprogrammed hour, the exterior lights would turn on. A house that barely needed people. The floors were wide-plank wood harvested from an old cotton mill in Utica, so flush there was nary a creak or complaint. The windows so clean that every month or so some common bird miscalculated, and perished broken-necked in the grass. Some efficient hands had been here, rolled up the blinds, turned down the thermostat, Windexed every surface, run the Dyson into the crevices of the sofa, picking up bits of organic blue corn tortilla chips and the errant dime. "This is nice."

Amanda took off her shoes at the door; she felt strongly about taking your shoes off at the door. "This is beautiful." The photographs on the website were a promise, and it was fulfilled: the pendant lamps hovering over the oak table, in case you wanted to do a jigsaw puzzle at night, the gray marble kitchen island where you could imagine kneading dough, the double sink beneath the window overlooking the pool, the stove with its copper faucet so you could fill up your pot without having to move it. The people who owned this house were rich enough to be thoughtful. She'd stand at that sink and soap up the dishes, while Clay stood just outside grilling, drinking a beer, a watchful eye on the children playing Marco Polo in the pool.

"I'll get the things." The subtext was clear; Clay was going to smoke a cigarette, a vice that was meant to be a secret but was not.

Amanda wandered through the place. There was a great room with a television, French doors out to the deck. There were two smallish bedrooms, color schemes of aqua and navy, Jack and Jill bath between them. There was a closet with beach towels and a stacked washer and dryer, there was a long hallway to the master bedroom, lined with inoffensive black-and-white beach scenes. Leaving aside tasteful, everything was thoughtful: a wooden box to hide the plastic bottle of laundry soap, a huge seashell cradling a cake of soap, still in its paper wrapper. The master bed was king-size, so massive it never would have rounded the stairwell to get into their third-floor apartment. The en suite bath was all white (tile, sink, towels, soap, a white dish of white seashells), that particular fantasy of purity to escape the reality of your own excrement. Extraordinary, and only $340 a day plus the cleaning fee and refundable security deposit. From the bedroom Amanda could see her children, already wiggled into their quick-drying Lycra, hurtling toward the placid blue. Archie, long limbs and acute angles, barely convex chest sprouting brown twists at the pink nipples; Rose, curvy and jiggling, downy with baby hair, her polka-dot one-piece straining just so at the legs, pudendum in relief. An anticipatory scream, then they met the water with that delicious clack. In the woods beyond, something started at the sound, fluttered up into view from the general brown of the scene: two fat turkeys, dumb and wild and annoyed at the intrusion. Amanda smiled.

3

Amanda volunteered to go to the grocery. They'd passed a store, and she retraced that path. She drove slowly, windows down.

The store was frigid, brightly lit, wide-aisled. She bought yogurt and blueberries. She bought sliced turkey, whole-grain bread, that pebbly mud-colored mustard, and mayonnaise. She bought potato chips and tortilla chips and jarred salsa full of cilantro, even though Archie refused to eat cilantro. She bought organic hot dogs and inexpensive buns and the same ketchup everyone bought. She bought cold, hard lemons and seltzer and Tito's vodka and two bottles of nine-dollar red wine. She bought dried spaghetti and salted butter and a head of garlic. She bought thick-cut bacon and a two-pound bag of flour and twelve-dollar maple syrup in a faceted glass bottle like a tacky perfume. She bought a pound of ground coffee, so potent she could smell it through the vacuum seal, and size 4 coffee filters made of recycled paper. If you care? She cared! She bought a three-pack of paper towels, and a spray-on sunscreen, and aloe, because the children had inherited their father's pale skin. She bought those fancy crackers you put out when there were guests, and Ritz crackers, which everyone liked best, and crumbly white cheddar cheese and extra-garlicky hummus and an unsliced hard salami and those carrots that are tumbled around until they're the size of a child's fingers. She bought packages of cookies from Pepperidge Farm and three pints of Ben & Jerry's politically virtuous ice cream and a Duncan Hines boxed mix for a yellow cake and a Duncan Hines tub of chocolate frosting with a red plastic lid, because parenthood had taught her that on a vacation's inevitable rainy day you could while away an hour by baking a boxed cake. She bought two tumescent zucchini, a bag of snap peas, a bouquet of curling kale so green it was almost black. She bought a bottle of olive oil and a box of Entenmann's crumb-topped doughnuts, a bunch of bananas and a bag of white nectarines and two plastic packages of strawberries, a dozen brown eggs, a plastic box of prewashed spinach, a plastic container of olives, some heirloom tomatoes wrapped in crinkling cellophane, marbled green and shocking orange. She bought three pounds of ground beef and two packages of hamburger buns, their bottoms dusty with flour, and a jar of locally made pickles. She bought four avocados and three limes and a sandy bundle of cilantro even though Archie refused to eat cilantro. It was more than two hundred dollars, but never mind.

"I'm going to need some help." The man placing every item into brown paper bags was maybe in high school but maybe not. He wore a yellow T-shirt and had brown hair and an overall square affect, like he'd been carved from a block of wood. There was some stirring, watching his hands at work, but vacations did that, didn't they, made you horny, made everything seem possible, a life completely different than the one you normally inhabited. She, Amanda, might be a mother temptress, sucking on a postadolescent's hot tongue in the parking lot of the Stop and Shop. Or she might just be another woman from the city spending too much money on too much food.

The boy, or maybe he was a man, put the bags into a cart and followed Amanda into the parking lot. He loaded them into the trunk, and she gave him a five-dollar bill.

She sat, the engine idling, to see if she had cell-phone service, and the endorphin rush of the arriving emails—Jocelyn, Jocelyn, Jocelyn, their agency director, one of the clients, two missives sent to the entire office by the head project manager—was almost as sexual as that flutter over the bag boy.

There was nothing important happening at work, but it was a relief to know that for certain rather than worry that there was. Amanda turned on the radio. She half recognized the song that was playing. She stopped at the gas station and bought Clay a pack of Parliaments. They were on vacation. That night, after hamburgers and hot dogs and grilled zucchini, after bowls of ice cream with cookies crumbled on top of them and maybe some sliced strawberries too, maybe they'd fuck—not make love, that was for home, fucking was for vacation, sweaty and humid and tantalizingly foreign in someone else's Pottery Barn sheets, then go outside, slip into that heated pool, and let the water wash them clean, and smoke one cigarette each and talk about what you talked about after you'd been married for as long as they'd been: finances, the children, fever dreams of real estate (How nice it would be to have a house like this all their own!). Or they'd talk about nothing, the other pleasure of a long marriage. They'd watch television. She drove back to the painted brick house.

4

C lay bound the towel around his waist. The gesture of opening double doors was inherently grand. It was cold inside, and very hot outside. The trees had been pruned to keep the shade from the pool. All that sun made you lightheaded. His damp feet left marks on the wooden floors. They melted away in seconds. Clay cut through the kitchen and out via the side door. He retrieved his cigarettes from the glove box, wincing at the gravel. He sat on the front lawn in the shade of a tree and smoked. He should feel bad about this, but tobacco was the foundation of the nation. Smoking tethered you to history itself! It was a patriotic act, or once had been, anyway, like owning slaves or killing the Cherokee.

It was pleasant to sit outside, near naked, the sun

and air on your skin reminding you that you're just another animal. He could have sat there nude. There were no other houses, there were no signs of human life, save an honor-system farm stand near a half mile back. There had been a time they'd been so naked together, Archie a wisp of bone and giggles sharing the tub with his parents, but you grew out of that unless you were a hippie.

He couldn't hear the children carrying on in the pool. The house between him and them was not so large, but the trees absorbed their noise as cotton might blood. Clay felt safe, cossetted, embraced, the rampart of hedge keeping the world at bay. As though he could see it, he pictured Amanda, adrift on an inflatable lounge, pretending dignity (hard to do: even the duck lacks that somehow, the water's undulations always ridiculous) and reading *Elle*. Clay unknotted the towel and lay back. The grass was itchy under his back. He stared at the sky. Without really thinking about it—but also kind of thinking about it—his right hand wandered down the front of his J.Crew suit, fumbled with his penis, gone cold and shy from the water. Vacations made you horny.

Clay felt light, unfettered, though he was not fettered by much. He was supposed to be reviewing a book for the *New York Times Book Review* and had brought his laptop. He only needed nine hundred words. In a couple of hours he'd put the family to bed, fill a tumbler with ice and vodka, sit shirtless on the deck, laptop illuminating the night, smoke cigarettes, and the thoughts would come and the nine hundred words would follow. Clay was diligent but also (he knew it) a little lazy. He wanted to be asked to write for the *New York Times Book Review* but didn't want to actually write anything.

Clay had tenure, and Amanda had the title of director, but they did not have level floors and central air-conditioning. The key to success was having parents who had succeeded. Still, they could pantomime ownership for a week. His penis jerked itself toward the sun, a yoga salutation, bouncing, then stiff at the house's allure. Marble countertops and a Miele washer and Clay had a full erection, his dick hovering over his belly like the searching needle in a compass.

Clay ground out his cigarette guiltily. He was never without breath mints or chewing gum. He tied the towel around his waist and went into the house. The garbage slid out on casters from beneath the countertops. Clay ran the butt under the faucet (imagine if he burned the house down?) then buried it in the refuse. There was lemon soap in a glass dispenser by the sink. From the window he could see his family. Rose was lost in a game of her own. Archie was doing pull-ups on the diving board, hoisting his skinny body heavenward, his bony shoulders the pink of undercooked meat.

Sometimes, looking at his family, he was flooded with this desire to *do* for them. I'll build you a house or knit you a sweater, whatever is required. Pursued by wolves? I'll make a bridge of my body so you can cross that ravine. They were all that mattered to him, but of course they didn't really understand that, because such was the parental contract. Clay found a baseball game on the radio, though he did not care about baseball. He thought the description comforting, the play-by-play like being read a bedtime story. Clay dumped two packages of the raw meat into a large bowl—Archie would eat three hamburgers—and diced a white onion, mixed that in, pinched in salt and ground in pepper, added Worcestershire sauce like daubing perfume onto a wrist. He molded the burgers and lined them up on a plate. Clay sliced cheddar cheese, halved the buns. The towel was slipping from his waist, so he washed the raw meat from his hands and tied it more tightly. He filled a glass bowl with potato chips and ferried the food outside. Every step felt familiar, like he'd been throwing together summertime meals in that kitchen all his life.

"Dinner in a bit," he called. No one acknowledged

this. Clay switched on the propane, used the long lighter to make the flame catch. Half naked, he tended the raw meat, thinking he must resemble a caveman, some long-forgotten ancestor. Who was to say that one hadn't stood once on that very spot? Millennia earlier or even just centuries, some shirtless Iroquois in hide loincloth, stoking a fire that the flesh of his flesh might dine on flesh. The thought made him smile.

5

They ate on the deck, in dishabille, an assemblage of towels in garish colors and ketchup-stained paper napkins. Hamburgers the size of hockey pucks inside airy bread. Rose was particularly susceptible to the tart charms of vinegar potato chips. Crumbs and grease on her chin. Amanda loved that Rose could still reach girlishness. Her mind was one thing, her body another: it was the hormones in the milk or the food chain or the water supply or the air or who knew.

It was so hot that the parents didn't even bid the children shower, let them sprawl on the gingham-upholstered sofa in their fleshy bodies, Archie lank and Rose lush: visible ribs and a constellation of moles, dimpled elbows and a downy chin. Rose wanted to watch a cartoon, and Archie was secretly comforted by animation—wistful for his own youth! His skin prickled in the air-conditioned chill, the unfamiliar sofa was soft, and his mind and mouth felt thick and slow from the day's heat or exertion. He was too tired to get up for another hamburger, gone cold, doused in ketchup, which he'd eat standing up in the kitchen, the tile cold underfoot. In a minute, he thought, but his body was pleading with hunger from those hours in the pool or maybe just the hours cooped up in the car, his body always felt this way.

Amanda went to shower. The thing was fixed in the ceiling, the water falling onto you as rain might. She set it as hot as possible to banish the residue of the SPF lotion. That stuff always felt vaguely poisonous, an ounce of prevention, etc. She wore her hair neither short nor long, without bangs, which made her look youthful in a way that was not good in an office environment. Two different kinds of vanity at odds—a desire to look capable rather than girlish. Amanda knew that she looked like the sort of woman she was. You could read it on her from a great distance. Her poise and posture, her clothes and grooming, all said who she was.

Her body still contained the secondhand warmth of the sun. The pool water had barely been a respite, the tepidity of bathwater. Amanda's limbs felt thick and superb. She wanted to lie down and roll away into sleep.

Her fingers strayed to the parts of herself where they felt best, in search not of some internal pleasure but something more cerebral: the confirmation that she, her shoulders, her nipples, her elbows, all of it, existed. What a marvel, to have a body, a thing that contained you. Vacation was for being returned to your body.

Amanda wrapped her hair into a white towel like a woman in a certain kind of film. She spread lotion across her skin, pulled on the loose cotton pants she favored in bed, summertime, and an old T-shirt with a logo that no longer meant anything to her. It was impossible to keep track of the provenance of all their earthly possessions. The shirt's cotton so worn that it shone. She felt alive and if not sexy, then sexual; the promise mattered more than the transaction. She still loved him, nothing like that, and he knew her body—it had been eighteen years, of course he knew it—but she was human, wouldn't have minded novelty.

She peeked out of the door to the living room. Her children looked dazed, fatted, odalisques on the couch. Her husband was bent over his phone.

"Bed in twenty minutes." Amanda gave Clay a suggestive look, then closed the door behind her. She stepped out of her pants and into the cool percale of the bed. She did not draw the curtains—let them watch, the deer, the owls, the stupid flightless turkeys—

admire Clay's still impressive latissimus dorsi (he rowed at the New York Sports Club twice weekly), which she loved to sink her fingers into, catch the pleasant stink of his hairy armpits, applaud the practiced flick of his tongue against her.

The house was too far from the world to offer cellular service, but there was WiFi, a preposterously long password (018HGF234WRH357XIO) to keep out whom—the deer, the owls, the stupid flightless turkeys? She tapped the glass, spelling it out, random as Ouija or the rosary, then the thing took and the emails arrived, piling the one atop the other. Forty-one! She felt so necessary, so missed, so *loved*.

In her personal account she learned that things were on sale, that the book club she'd been meaning to join was scheduling a fall get-together, that the *New Yorker* had written about a Bosnian filmmaker. In her work account, there were questions, there were concerns, and people were seeking Amanda's participation, her opinion, her guidance. Everyone had received her out-of-office reply, sunny and authoritative, but she broke the promise to be in touch upon her return. No, don't do X. Yes, email Y. Ask so-and-so about such-and-such. Just a reminder to follow up with that person about this matter.

Her arm grew tingly from the exertion of holding

aloft the too-small phone. She flipped onto her stomach, the sheets warm from her body, so the transitive warmth against her vulva was that of her own body, and flopping around in the bed was an act of masturbation. She felt clean, ready to feel dirty, but she worked her way through the emails, distracting herself until at last Clay came to her, smelling of furtive cigarettes and the lemon wedges in his vodka.

The heat from the shower had softened her spine the way room temperature does a stick of butter. The occasional vinyasa class had made her more attentive to her bones. She let them give. She relaxed away from her usual resolve not to do the filthiest things they could conjure between the two of them. She let him knead his fingers into her hair and hold her head firmly but gently against the pillow, her throat a passage, a void to be filled. She let herself moan more loudly than she might have at home, because there was that long hall between them and the children's rooms. She bucked her hips back and up to meet his mouth, and later—it felt an eternity but was only twenty minutes—she took his wilting penis into her mouth, marveling at the taste of her own body.

"Christ." Clay was wheezing.

"You have to quit smoking." She worried about a

cardiac event. They were not so young. Every mother had contemplated the loss of a child; Amanda had no emotions left around the theoretical death of her husband. She'd love again, she told herself. He was a good man.

"I do." Clay did not mean it. There was already so little pleasure in modern life.

Amanda stood, stretched, happily sticky, wanting a cigarette herself; the dizzying effect would put her at some remove from what they had just done, which you needed after sex, even with a familiar. That wasn't really me! She opened the door, and the night was shocking with noise. Crickets or whatever bug that was, various maybe sinister footfalls in the dried leaves of the woods beyond the lawn, the stealthy breeze moving everything, maybe the vegetal growth actually made a sound, even, the barest *scritch, scritch* of the advancing grass, the heartbeat throb of the oak leaves flowing with chlorophyll.

Amanda had a feeling like being watched, but there was no one out there watching her, was there? An involuntary shiver at the very idea, then a retreat into the adult illusion of safety.

The two of them crept, naked as Neanderthals, across the deck, the only light a slice of it falling through the glass door. Clay heaved the cover off the hot tub, and they sank into its froth, the steam obscuring his glasses, a satisfied sensual grin. Her eyes adjusted to the darkness. His pale flesh in stark relief. She could see him as he was, but she loved him.

6

No one had bought cereal. Archie wanted a specific taste less than the feel of processed grain gone soft enough in milk. He yawned.

"Sorry, champ. I'll make you an omelet." His dad had this stupid game of being the best at making breakfast. Though he was a good cook—he always put butter on the toast and then put it back into the toaster oven so it melted into the bread until the thing was sloppy like someone had already chewed it—there was something sad in the way he needed attention for it.

Amanda was spreading sunscreen on Rose's back. The television was on, but no one was actually watching it. She wiped her hands on her own bare legs and put the bottle into the tote bag. "Rose, you're bringing three books? For one afternoon at the beach?"

"We'll be gone all day. What if I run out of something to read?"

"The bag is already very heavy—"

Rose didn't want to whine, it just sort of happened.

"You can put them in this bag." Clay thought the girl's bookishness reflected well on them. "Archie, can you bring this bag?"

"I need to go to the bathroom." Archie lingered in there before the mirror. He was wearing his lacrosse shirt, the one he'd cut the sleeves off because he wanted people to see his muscles, and he studied them, happy with what he saw.

"Hurry up," Clay called to his son, the irritation that necessitated this relaxation.

"I've got lunch in there. And water. And the blanket and towels." Amanda was pointing at bags, sure they'd forget something even so, best-laid plans.

"I've got it, I've got it." A little *Christ* under the breath, which was more a reflex than he realized. Archie took the bag his father had left by the sofa. It weighed nothing! He was so strong.

The family trooped outside, loaded their things, and buckled their bodies. The GPS churned, unable to locate itself, or them, or the rest of the world. Without much thinking about it, Clay found the road to the highway and the satellite recovered its hold on them and they drove under its protective gaze. The highway turned into a bridge that seemed to lead to nothing, that led to the end of America itself. They wound into the empty parking lot (it was early) and paid five dollars to a khaki-uniformed teen who seemed himself made of sand—golden curls, freckles, browned skin, teeth like little shells.

There was a tunnel from the lot to the shore that carried them past a park, flagpoles towering as redwoods, flags of many nations cracking in the ocean air.

"What's this?" Archie, derisive even when he didn't mean to be.

They stood in flip-flopped feet in a little canyon of concrete, and Amanda read the inscription. "It's for the victims of Flight 800." TWA, bound for Paris. Everyone had perished. You heard that rendered as souls, sometimes, which made it sound more grand or old-fashioned or sanctified. Amanda remembered— conspiracy theorists said it had been an American missile, but logic said it was mechanical failure. We pretend otherwise, but these things happen.

"Let's go!" Rose tugged on the tote bag slung across her father's shoulder.

It was hot but the wind was relentless, bringing in a chill from the void of the ocean. There was something Arctic in it, and who was to say that wasn't literally the case. The world was vast but also small and governed by logic. Amanda struggled to spread the blanket, something she'd found on the internet, block-printed by illiterate Indian villagers. She placed a bag at each corner to weigh the thing down. The children shed their layers and bounded off like gazelles. Rose investigated the detritus washed up on the sand, shells and plastic cups and iridescent balloons that had celebrated proms and sweet sixteens miles away. Archie knelt in the sand some distance from their encampment, pretending not to stare at the lifeguards, hale girls, sun-lightened locks and red swimsuits.

Amanda had a novel she could barely follow, with a tiresome central metaphor involving birds. Clay had the kind of book he normally had, a slender and unclassifiable critique of the way we live now, the sort of thing it's impossible to read near naked in the sun but important to have read, for his work.

His glance kept straying to the lifeguards. So did Amanda's. How could they not? There was a metaphor less tiresome—what would stand between you and death at the hands of nature but beautiful youth, flat stomachs, nipples the size of quarters, swollen biceps, hairless legs, browned skin, dry hair, mouths perfected by orthodontia, unquestioning eyes behind cheap plastic sunglasses?

They ate turkey sandwiches and chips that kept breaking off in the pasty guacamole (a smaller portion without the acrid herb, for the doted-upon son), then watermelon, bracing and cold. Archie slept, and Rose read one of her graphic novels. Archie woke and goaded his father into the waves, which were terrifying. Amanda watched for sharks because she had heard there were sharks. What would one of those teenage lifeguards do if there were sharks?

It was pleasant, it was diverting, it was exhausting. The sun was not waning, but the wind was winning. "We should go." Amanda packed their empty plastic containers back into the insulated bag she'd found in the kitchen. It was in precisely the spot where you'd store an insulated bag in your kitchen (a cabinet beneath the microwave).

Rose shivered, and her father wrapped her up in a towel just as he had when she'd been a toddler fresh from the bath. The family trudged back to their car, strangely defeated, and drove back across the bridge.

"There's a Starbucks." Amanda pressed her hand onto her husband's right forearm, excited.

He pulled in to the lot, and Amanda went inside. Alee, away from that wind, the air was still hot. The shop was the same as all locations of a chain tend to be, but wasn't that comforting? The signature colors, those dependable brown napkins—always a stack in the car for blowing winter noses or mopping up spills—the green plastic straws, the heavyset devotees paying seven dollars for cream-topped milkshakes in cups the size of athletic trophies. She ordered black coffees, though it was after three and it would keep her up late, or maybe it wouldn't, because proximity to the ocean always made her so tired.

There was a desultory de-sanding of limbs, using the backyard hose. Archie sprayed the thing directly down the front of his suit, his balls shellacked with actual tiny shells, then figured that was good enough and dove into the pool. He rubbed his scalp and could feel sand being dislodged, drifting away into the water.

Amanda washed her feet and then went inside to shower. The house felt reassuringly familiar after fewer than twenty-four hours. She played a podcast on the computer—something to do with the mind, she barely paid attention to it—and shampooed her hair again, hating the effect of the salt water on it. She dressed and found Clay whistling as he rinsed the sandy Tupperware.

"I'll make pasta," Amanda said.

"The kids are in the pool. I'm going to run to the store and get some cereal for Archie." He meant he'd run to the store, smoke a cigarette in the parking lot, go inside, wash his hands, come back with a hundred dollars' worth of food. "They're saying it might rain tomorrow."

"You can almost feel it." A promise in the air, or maybe it was a threat. She had brought her computer into the kitchen with her so she could keep listening to the podcast. She set it on the counter. "Get something sweet? Like . . . a pie. Get a pie. And maybe some more ice cream?" The night before, postcoital and woozy from the hot tub, they'd eaten an entire pint between the two of them. "Maybe some tomatoes. Another watermelon. Some berries. I don't know, whatever looks good."

He kissed her, an unfamiliar thing to do when running out on a simple errand, but sweet.

The window meant that she could watch the children as she did something else. She zested the lemon, dumped that into the softening butter, minced garlic and added that. She used the kitchen shears to hack at the parsley, which had a sharp and astonishing smell. She folded this all together into a thick paste. The hot pasta would dull the taste of the garlic.

She used the pot filler over the stove, helped herself to the kosher salt in the pantry, poured a glass of red wine. It made her stomach churn, red wine over black coffee. The water boiled. Her attention had drifted.

Beyond the pool, through the woods at the property's perimeter, Amanda saw a deer, then adjusted her eyes and saw two more, smaller. Mother and children! Wasn't that fitting. The animals were cautious, nosing through the brush in search of—what did deer eat? Her ignorance embarrassed her.

She strained the cooked pasta, dropped the herbed butter into the nest of noodles, replaced the lid, and opened the glass door. The air had grown cooler. It would rain, or something would happen, and they would have to spend the next day inside the house. There were board games, there was the television, maybe they'd watch a movie, there was a glass canister of dried corn in the pantry, maybe they'd pop some, lie about all day.

"It's time to come inside, guys."

Archie and Rose were in the hot tub, pink as cooking lobsters.

Amanda insisted the children bathe and banish that chlorine smell. She poured herself another glass of wine. Clay returned with a surprising number of paper bags.

"I went a little overboard." He looked sheepish. "I thought it might rain. I don't want to have to leave the house tomorrow."

Amanda frowned because she felt she was supposed

to. It wouldn't ruin them to spend a little more than was usual on groceries. Or maybe it was the wine. "Fine, fine. Put those away and let's eat?" She wasn't sure she wasn't slurring a little bit.

She laid the table. The children, redolent of marzipan (Dr. Bronner's, in the green bottle), sat. They were the best kind of tired, docile, almost polite, no burping or name-calling. Archie even helped his father clear the table, and Amanda lay on the sofa beside Rose, her head in her child's warm lap. She didn't mean to sleep, but she did, full of wine and pasta and bored by the television's prattle. Amanda was perplexed when she was roused twenty minutes on by an especially shrill commercial and Rose's need for the bathroom. Her mouth was dry.

"Have a nice nap?" Clay was teasing, not amorous (he was still sated) but romantic—even better or rarer. They'd made a nice life for themselves, hadn't they?

Amanda did the *New York Times* crossword on her phone—she was afraid of dementia, and felt this was preventative—and the time passed strangely, as it did when measured in minutes before the television. If the night before she'd been eager to look at her work and fuck her husband, tonight it felt important to linger on the sofa with her children, Archie dopey in his too-big hooded sweatshirt, Rose infantile, wrapped in the itchy woolen throw left on the sofa's arm. Clay served bowls of ice cream, then collected the bowls, and the dishwasher ran with its reassuring gurgle, and Rose's eyes looked blank and Archie yawned loudly, suddenly, so like a man, and Amanda sent the children to bed, telling them to brush their teeth but not standing sentry to verify that they did.

She yawned, was tired enough to go to bed, but knew somehow that if she moved, she would not fall asleep. Clay changed the channel, pausing a moment on Rachel Maddow and then switching to a thriller that neither of them were able to follow, detectives and their prey.

"Television is idiotic." Clay turned it off. He'd rather play with his phone. He dropped some ice into a glass. "You want a drink?"

Amanda shook her head. "I'm done."

She didn't yet quite know which switch controlled which light. She flicked one, and the pool and the grounds beyond it were illuminated, pure white beams shot through the green branches overhead. She turned the light off, returning things to their black state, which seemed right, seemed natural.

"I need some water," she said or thought, and made her way into the kitchen. She was filling one of the

IKEA glasses when she heard a scratch, a footfall, a voice, something that felt odd or wrong. "Did you hear that?"

Clay mumbled; he wasn't truly listening. He checked the little buttons on the side of his phone to make sure the sound was turned off. "It's not me."

"No." She sipped her water. "It was something else."

There it was again: shuffle, a voice, a quiet murmur, a *presence*. A disruption, a change. Something. This time Amanda was more certain. Her heart quickened. She felt sober, awake. She put her cup down on the marble counter, quietly—suddenly that seemed right, to move stealthily.

"I heard something." She was whispering.

Such moments, Clay was called upon. He had to be the man. He didn't mind it. Maybe he liked it. Maybe it made him feel necessary. From down the hall, he could almost hear Archie, snoring like a sleeping dog. "It's probably just a deer in the front garden."

"It's something." Amanda held up a hand to silence him. Her mouth was metallic with fear. "I know I heard something."

There it was, undeniable: noise. A cough, a voice, a step, a hesitation, that uncategorizable animal knowledge that there's another of the species nearby and the pause, pregnant, to see if they mean harm. There was a knock at the door. A knock at the door of this house, where no one knew they were, not even the global positioning system, this house near the ocean but also lost in farmland, this house of red bricks painted white, the very material the smartest little piggy chose because it would keep him safest. There was a knock at the door.

7

What were they supposed to do?

Amanda stood, frozen, a prey's instinct. Gather your thoughts. "Get a bat." That old solution: violence.

"A bat?" Clay pictured the flying mammal. "A bat?" He understood, then, but where would he get a bat? When had he last held a bat? Did they even have a baseball bat at home, and if they did, had they brought it on vacation? No, but when had they decided to forsake that American diversion? In their foyer on Baltic Street they had a clutch of umbrellas of varying degrees of broken, an extra windshield scraper, Archie's lacrosse stick, some of those circulars, never asked for, a sheaf of coupons in rainproof plastic that would never biodegrade. Well, lacrosse was from the Indians, maybe that was more all-American. On a console table, beneath a framed photograph of Coney Island, there was a brass object, an artful little torque, the kind of made-in-China geegaw meant to add character to hotel rooms or model apartments. He picked it up but found it weighed nothing. Besides, what would he do, wrap his fingers around it, strike some stranger in the head? He was a professor.

"I don't know." Her whisper was built for the stage. Surely whoever was on the other side of the door could hear her. "Who could it be?"

This was ridiculous. "I don't know." Clay put the little objet d'art back in its place. Art could not protect them.

There was another knock at the door. This time, a man's voice. "I'm sorry. Hello?"

Clay could not imagine a killer could be so polite. "It's nothing. I'll get it."

"No!" Amanda had this terrible flash of feeling, a premonition if the worst came to pass and passing paranoia if it did not. She did not like this.

"Let's just calm down." Maybe he was unconsciously channeling behaviors seen in films. He looked at his wife until she seemed to calm, like what tamers did with their lions, dominance and eye contact. He didn't entirely believe in the act. "Get the phone. Just in case." That was decisive and smart; he was proud of himself for having thought of it.

Amanda went into the kitchen. There was a desk, a cordless telephone, a 516 number. In her lifetime the cordless telephone had been both innovation and obsolete. They still had one at home, but no one ever used it. She picked it up. Should she press the button, dial the nine and then the one and wait?

Clay unbolted the lock and pulled open the door. What was he expecting?

The interrogatory light of the porch revealed a man, black, handsome, well proportioned though maybe a little short, in his sixties, with a warm smile. It was funny, how quickly the eye could register: benign, or harmless, or instantly reassuring. He wore a rumpled blazer, a loosened knit tie, a striped shirt, those brown pants every man over thirty-five wears. He held up his hands in a gesture that was either conciliatory or said *Don't shoot.* By his age, black men were adept at this gesture.

"I'm so sorry to bother you." He sounded as people rarely did when saying those words: sincere. He knew how to put on an act.

"Hello?" Clay said it as if he was answering a telephone. Opening a door to an unexpected visitor was without precedent. Urban life contained only the guy who came to deliver an Amazon box, and he had to buzz first. "Hi?"

"I'm so sorry to bother you." The man's voice was gravelly with the gravitas of a news anchor. This quality, he knew, made him sound more sincere.

Beside but just behind the man was a woman, also black, also of an indeterminate age, in boxy linen skirt and jacket. "*We're* sorry," she corrected, an italicized *we*; it was so practiced that she had to be his wife. "We didn't mean to frighten you."

Clay laughed as though the idea were ridiculous. Frightened, he was not frightened. She looked like the kind of woman you'd see in a television ad for an osteoporosis medication.

Amanda lingered between the foyer and the kitchen, behind a column, as if this provided some tactical advantage. She was not persuaded. An emergency call might be in order. People in ties could be criminals. She had not gone to lock the children's bedroom doors; what kind of mother was she?

"Can I help you?" Was that what one said in such a circumstance? Clay was unclear.

The man cleared his throat. "We're sorry to bother you." A third time, an incantation. He went on. "I know it's late. A knock at the door, way out here." He had imagined how this would transpire. He had re-hearsed his part.

Now the woman picked it up: "We couldn't decide if we should knock at the front door or the side door." She laughed to show how absurd this was. Her voice carried, implied long-ago elocution lessons. A trace of Hepburn that sounded like aristocracy. "I thought this might be less frightening—"

Clay protested too much. "Not frightening, just surprising."

"Of course, of course." The man had expected as much. "I said we should try the side door. It's glass, so you could have seen us and known that we're just—" He trailed off, a shrug to say *We mean you no harm.*

"I thought that might be stranger, though. Or frightening." The woman tried to catch Clay's eye.

Their near-unison seemed charming to the point of comedy, like Powell and Loy. Clay's adrenaline fermented into annoyance. "Can we . . . help you?" He hadn't even heard their car, if they had come by car, but how else would they have come?

Clay had said *we,* and so, telephone tight in her hand like a child's favored plush toy, Amanda stepped into the foyer. They were probably lost motorists, or had a flat tire. Occam's razor and all that. "Hi!" She forced in some cheer, as though she'd been waiting for them.

"Good evening." The man wanted to underscore that he was a gentleman. That was part of the plan.

"You startled us. We weren't expecting anyone." Amanda didn't mind admitting it. She calculated that it might establish her upper hand. She thought it might say *This is our house, now what do you want?*

There was wind, and it sounded like a chorus of voices. The trees swayed, their heads tossed with abandon. A storm was coming or out there somewhere.

The woman shivered. Her linen clothes could not keep her warm. She seemed pitiable, elderly, ill prepared. She was smart, and she'd been counting on this.

Clay could not help feeling bad, or rude. The woman was old enough to be his mother, though his own mother was long dead. Good manners were a tool that helped you deal with moments this strange. "You caught us by surprise. But what can we do for you?"

The black man looked at Amanda, and his smile warmed further. "Well, you must be Amanda. Right? Amanda. I'm sorry, but—" The breeze eddied around them, through their summer clothes. He said her name a third time because he knew it would be effective. "Amanda, do you think we could come inside?"

8

Recognizing people was one of Amanda's skills. She bought cocktails for the apparatchiks from Minneapolis and Columbus and St. Louis who paid her. She remembered who was who and asked after their families. This was a point of pride. She looked at the man and saw only a black man she had never seen before.

"You know one another!" Clay was reassured. The breeze raised the hair on his legs.

"We've not had the pleasure of meeting face-to-face." The man had the practice of a salesman which was, ultimately, what he was. "I'm G. H."

The letters meant nothing to her. Amanda couldn't figure whether he was trying to spell something.

"George." The woman thought the name more

gentle than the initials, and this was a moment when they needed to seem human. You never knew who had guns and was ready to stand their ground. "He's George."

He thought of himself as George. He spoke of himself as G. H. "—George, right, I'm George. This is our house."

Possession was some fraction of the law, and Amanda had deluded herself. She'd been pretending that this was their house! "I'm sorry?"

"This is our house," he said again. "We emailed back and forth—about the house?" He tried to sound firm but also gentle.

Amanda remembered, then: GHW@washington groupfund.com—the formal opacity of those initials. The place was comfortable but sufficiently anonymous that she had not bothered to try to picture its owners, and now, seeing them, she knew that if she had bothered to picture them, her picture would have been incorrect. This didn't seem to her like the sort of house where black people lived. But what did she mean by that? "This is—your house?"

Clay was disappointed. They were paying for the illusion of ownership. They were on vacation. He closed the door, leaving the world out there, where it belonged.

"We're so sorry to bother you." Ruth still had her hand on George's shoulder. Well, they were inside; they'd accomplished something.

Why had Clay closed the door, invited these people in? It was so like him. He always wanted to handle the business of life but was not fully prepared to do so. Amanda wanted proof. She wanted to inspect the mortgage, a photo ID. These people and their disheveled clothes could be—well, they looked more like evangelists than criminals, hopeful pamphleteers come to witness Jehovah.

"You gave us a bit of a fright!" Clay didn't mind confessing his own cowardice, since it had passed. *A bit* barely counted, and it was, importantly, their fault. "Goodness, it's cold out all of a sudden."

"It is." G. H. was as good as anyone at predicting how other people would behave. But it took time. They were inside. That was what mattered. "Summer storm? Maybe it'll pass."

They were four adults standing about awkwardly as in those last anticipatory moments at an orgy.

Amanda was furious at everyone, Clay most of all. She twitched, certain one of these people would produce a gun, a knife, a demand. She wished she'd still been holding the telephone, though who could say how long it would take for the local precinct to get to their beautiful house in the deep of the woods. She didn't even say anything.

G. H. was ready. He had prepared, tried to guess how these people might react. "I understand how strange it must be for you, us turning up like this unannounced."

"Unannounced." Amanda inspected the word, and it didn't hold up to scrutiny.

"We'd have called, you see, but the phones—"

They'd have called? Did these people have her number?

"I'm Ruth." She extended a hand. Every couple apportioned labor by strength, even or especially at such moments. Her role was to shake hands and make nice and put these people at ease so they could get what they wanted.

"Clay." He shook her hand.

"And you're Amanda." Ruth smiled.

Amanda took the stranger's manicured hand. If calluses meant honest labor, did softness imply dishonesty? "Yes," she said.

"And I'm G. H., again. Clay, nice to meet you."

Clay applied more pressure than he normally might have, as he had a point to prove.

"And Amanda, it's nice to meet face-to-face."

Amanda crossed arms over her chest. "Yes. Though

I have to admit that I wasn't expecting to meet you at all."

"No, of course not."

"Maybe we should—sit?" It was their house, what was Clay supposed to do?

"That would be lovely." Ruth had the smile of a politician's wife.

"Sit? Yes. Fine." Amanda tried to communicate something to her husband, but one look couldn't contain it. "Maybe in the kitchen. We'll have to be quiet, though, the children are sleeping."

"The children. Of course. I hope we didn't wake them." G. H. should have guessed there would be children, but maybe that helped the situation.

"Archie could sleep through a nuclear bomb. I'm sure they're fine." Clay was his usual joking self.

"I think I'll just go check on them." Amanda was icy, and tried to imply that it was her habit to peer in at her sleeping children every so often.

"They're fine." Clay couldn't understand what she was up to.

"I'm just going to go check on them. Why don't you—" She didn't know how to complete the thought, and so she did not bother.

"Let's sit." Clay gestured at the stools at the kitchen island.

"Clay, I should explain." G. H. took this on as a masculine burden, like arranging rental cars for trips out of town. He thought another husband might understand. "As I said, I would have called. We tried to, actually, but there's no service."

"We stayed not far from here a couple of summers ago." Clay wanted to establish that he had some hold on this geography. That he knew what it was like to have a house in the country. "Impossible to get a signal most of the time."

"That's true," G. H. said. He had sat, put elbows on marble, leaned forward. "But I'm not sure if that's what's happening at the moment."

"How's that?" Clay felt he should offer them something. Weren't they guests? Or was he the guest? "Can I get you some water?"

Down the dark hall, Amanda used her cell phone as a light. Having confirmed that Archie and Rose still existed, lost in the unworried sleep of children, she tarried just out of sight, straining to hear what was being discussed while trying to get her phone to engage. She gazed at it as if it were a mirror, but it did not recognize her—maybe the hallway was too dark— and did not come to life. Amanda pressed the home button, and it lit up, showing her a news alert, the barely legible *T* of the *New York Times* and only a few words: "Major blackout reported on the East Coast of the United States." She jabbed at it, but the application did not open, just the white screen of the thinking machine. This was a specific flavor of irritation. She couldn't be mad, but she was.

"Tonight we were at the symphony." G. H. was in the middle of his explanation. "In the Bronx."

"He's on the board of the Philharmonic—" Connubial pride, it couldn't be helped. She and George believed in giving back. "It's to encourage people to take an interest in classical music . . ." Ruth was over-explaining.

Amanda came into the room.

"The kids are okay?" Clay did not understand that this had been only pretense.

"They're fine." Amanda wanted to show her husband her phone. She didn't have any news beyond those eleven words, but it was something, and represented some advantage over these people.

"We were driving back to the city. Home. Then something happened." He wasn't trying to be vague. Even in the car he and Ruth hadn't spoken of it, because they were afraid.

"A blackout." Amanda produced this, triumphant.

"How did you know?" G. H. was surprised. He had expected to have to explain. They'd seen nothing but darkness all the way out, and then, through the trees, the glow of their own house. They couldn't believe it because it didn't make sense, but they didn't care to make sense. The relief of light and its safety.

"A blackout?" Clay was expecting something worse.

"I got a news alert." Amanda took her phone from her pocket and put it on the counter.

"What did it say?" Ruth wanted more information. She'd seen it with her own eyes but knew nothing. "Did it say why?"

"Just that. There was a blackout on the East Coast." She looked at the phone again, but the alert was gone, and she didn't know how to return to it.

"It is windy outside." Clay felt that the cause and effect was clear.

"It's hurricane season. Wasn't there news about a hurricane?" Amanda couldn't recall.

"A blackout." G. H. nodded. "So we thought. Well, we live on the fourteenth floor."

"The traffic lights would have all gone out. It would have been chaos." Ruth didn't want to bother explaining in more detail. The city was as unnatural as it was possible to be, accretion of steel and glass and capital, and light was fundamental to its existence. A city without power was like a flightless bird, an accident of evolution.

"A blackout?" Clay felt like he was simply offering the word to someone who had forgotten it. "There's been a blackout. That doesn't seem so bad."

Amanda didn't buy it. It didn't seem true. "The lights seem to be working here."

She was right, of course. Still, everyone looked at the pendants over the kitchen island, like four people seeking hypnosis. You couldn't explain electricity at all, neither its presence nor its absence. Were her words an act of hubris? There was the sound of the wind against the window over the sink. Immediately thereafter, the lights flickered. Not once nor twice; four times, like a message in Morse that they had to decipher, like a succession of flashbulbs, but it held steady, it held course, the light held the night at bay. The four of them had breathed in sharply; all four of them exhaled.

9

"Jesus Christ." The Lord's name in vain meant blasphemy but also futility. Jesus cared nothing for Clay, but the power didn't go out. Clay had already imagined Amanda and the other woman (what was her name?) screaming. Maybe it was unkind to equate femininity with fear. He'd have to reason with them— a windy night, a far-off corner of Long Island. The world was so big that much of it was remote. You could forget this if you lived too long in a city. Electricity was a miracle. They should be grateful.

"It's fine." G. H. said it to himself, to his wife.

"So there was a blackout, and you drove all the way out here?" Amanda couldn't make sense of this. Manhattan was so far away. It didn't make any sense.

"These roads—they're familiar. I barely even

thought about it. We saw the lights go, and I looked at Ruth." G. H. didn't know how he would explain what he didn't entirely understand.

"We thought we might stay," Ruth said. No sense dancing around it. Ruth had always been direct.

"You thought you might stay—here?" Amanda knew these people wanted something. "But we're staying here."

"We knew we couldn't drive into the city. We knew we couldn't walk up fourteen flights. So we drove out here and thought you might understand."

"Of course." Clay understood.

Amanda looked at her husband. "What he means is, of course we *understand*—" Did she, though? What if this was some con? Perfect strangers worming their way into the house, into their lives.

"I know it's a surprise. But maybe you can . . . This is our house. We wanted to be in our house. Safe. While we figured out what's going on out there." G. H. was being honest, but it still seemed like he was selling something.

"It's our good luck we had gas." Ruth nodded. "Honestly, I don't know how much farther we could go."

"Aren't there any hotels . . ." Amanda was trying not to be rude, but she knew this sounded rude. "We've rented the house."

Clay was thinking it over. He began to say something. He was persuaded.

"Of course! You've rented the house." G. H. knew they'd talk about money, because most conversations got there eventually. Money was his subject. It was no matter. "We could of course offer you something. We know it's an inconvenience."

"You know, we're on vacation." Amanda thought *inconvenience* too mild a word. It felt like a euphemism. That he'd been so quick to bring money into it seemed more dishonest.

G. H. had silvered hair, tortoiseshell glasses, a gold watch. He had presence. He sat higher in his seat. "Clay. Amanda." This was something he'd learned at business school (in Cambridge): when to deploy first names. "I could absolutely refund you your money."

"You want us to leave? In the middle of the night? My children are sleeping. And you just come in here and start talking about refunding our money? I should call the company, can you even do that?" Amanda walked to the living room to get her computer. "Maybe there's a phone number on the website—"

"I'm not saying you should leave!" G. H. laughed. "We can refund you say, fifty percent of what you paid? You know, there's an in-law suite. We'll stay downstairs."

LEAVE THE WORLD BEHIND • 63

"Fifty percent?" Clay liked the promise of a less expensive vacation.

"I really think we ought to look at the terms and conditions—" Amanda opened the laptop. "Of course it's not working now. Maybe the WiFi needs to be reset?"

"Let me try." Clay reached toward his wife's computer.

"I don't need your help, Clay." She did not like the implication of her inability. They both had a proximity to youth—college kids for him, for Amanda an assistant and junior staff. They'd both been subject to that humiliating inversion: watching, gleaning, imitating, like toddlers playing at dressing up. Once you were past a certain age, this was how you learned—you had to master technology or be mastered by it. "It's not connected."

"We heard the emergency broadcast system." Ruth thought this explained a great deal. "I thought to turn on the radio. 'This is the emergency broadcast system.'" Her tone was not mocking but faithful, sounding the right stresses and intonation. "Not 'a test.' Do you understand? Not 'This is only a test.' That's the only way I've ever heard it, so I didn't even notice at first, then I kept listening and I heard it again, again, again, 'This is the emergency broadcast system.'"

"Emergency?" Amanda was trying to be logical. "But of course, a blackout is a kind of emergency."

"Surely. That's one of the reasons we thought it best to just come home. It could be unsafe out there." G. H. rested his case.

"Well, we have a lease agreement." Amanda invoked the law. Fine, at the moment that document was filed away in cyberspace, a shelf they could not reach. Also the whole business felt off in some way she could not explain.

"May I?" G. H. pushed his stool back and walked to the desk. He took the car keys from his blazer pocket and unlocked a drawer. He produced an envelope, the sort provided by a bank, and flipped through the currency inside it. "We could give you a thousand dollars now, for the night? That would cover almost half of what you're paying for the week, I think?"

Clay tried not to, but he always felt moved in a very particular way by the sight of lots of money. He wanted to count it. Had that envelope just been in a drawer in the kitchen all this time? He wanted a cigarette. "A thousand dollars?"

"There is an emergency outside." Ruth wanted to remind them of this. It seemed amoral to have to pay them, but she hadn't expected anything else.

"It's up to you." G. H. knew how to persuade someone. "Of course. We would be very grateful. We could
show you how grateful we are. Then, tomorrow, we'll
know a little more. We'll figure it out." He did not
commit to leaving, which was important.

Clay continued to prod his wife's work-issued computer. "This doesn't seem to be responding." His in-
tention had been pure. He wanted to be the one to
show them that the world was chugging along, that
people were still photographing their Aperol spritzes
and tweeting invective about the mismanaged public
transport system. In the minutes since that news alert
had been issued, some intrepid reporter had likely figured the whole thing out. He could still hear the wind
that he blamed. It was always some innocent thing.
"Anyway. I think one night—"

"Perhaps we could discuss this privately." Amanda
did not want to leave these people unattended.

"Right. Of course." G. H. nodded like this was the
most sensible thing. He put the fat little envelope down
on the counter.

"Yeah." Clay was flustered. He didn't know what
there was to discuss besides that bundle of money.
"Maybe we'll just go into the other room?"

"Say, you wouldn't mind if we have a drink?"

Clay shook his head.

G. H. used the keys once more, unlocking a tall cabinet by the sink. He rummaged around inside.

"We'll be right back. Make yourself—" Amanda didn't finish the sentence because it seemed silly to.

10

It was colder in the master bedroom, or the chill was something they carried with them.

"Why would you tell them they could stay?" She was angry.

Clay thought it was perfectly obvious. "There's been a blackout. They got scared. They're *old*." He whispered this, felt that it was disrespectful to point out.

"They're strangers." She said it like he was an idiot. Had no one ever warned Clay about strangers?

"Well, they introduced themselves."

"They just knocked on the door in the middle of the night." Amanda couldn't believe they were discussing this.

"Well, it's better than if they'd just burst in the door—" Wasn't that their right?

"They scared the shit out of me." Now that fear had passed, Amanda could admit to it. It was an insult. The temerity of these people—to scare her!

"They scared me too." Clay was downplaying it. It was in the past. "But they're just a little frightened themselves, I think. They didn't know what else to do."

Their onetime therapist had long ago urged Amanda not to be angry when Clay failed to act as she might have. People could not be blamed for being who they were! Still, she faulted him for it. Clay was too easily taken, too reluctant to stand up for himself. "Here's an idea. Go to a hotel."

"It is their house." These beautiful rooms seemed like theirs but weren't. You had to respect that, Clay thought.

"We rented it." Amanda was whispering still. "What are the kids going to say?"

Clay couldn't imagine what the children would say or whether they would say anything. The kids cared only for what directly affected them, and they let very little affect them. The presence of strangers might mean better behavior, but even that couldn't be counted upon. The children might bicker, swear, burp, sing, no matter who might overhear.

"What if they murder us?" Amanda felt her husband was not paying attention.

"Why would they murder us?"

This was harder to answer. "Why does anyone murder anyone? I don't know. Satanic ritual? Some weird fetish? Revenge? I don't know!"

Clay laughed. "They're not here to murder us."

"Don't you read the news?"

"This was in the news? Elderly black murderers are roaming Long Island, preying on unsuspecting vacationers?"

"We didn't ask for any *proof.* I didn't even hear their car, did you?"

"I didn't. But it's windy. We were watching television. Maybe we just didn't hear it?"

"And maybe they snuck up the road. To—I don't know. To cut our throats."

"I think we should just calm down—"

"It's a con."

"You think they sent a fraudulent news alert to your cell phone? They're more sophisticated criminals than I'd have guessed."

"It just feels a little improvised, is all. And suspicious. They want to stay here, with us? I don't like it. Rose is just down the hall. A strange man. What if he sneaks in there and— I don't want to think about it."

"You don't think he'd molest Archie, though. Amanda, listen to yourself."

"She's a girl, okay? I'm a mother, I'm supposed to be protective. And I just don't like the way the whole thing sounds. I don't even think this is their house."

"He had the keys."

"He did." She lowered her voice still more. "What if he's the handyman? What if she's the maid? What if this is just a scam, and the blackout or whatever is just a coincidence?" She was at least appropriately ashamed by her conjecture. But those people didn't look like the sort to own such a beautiful house. They might, though, clean it.

"He took that envelope out of that drawer."

"Sleight of hand. How do you know that drawer was locked? Maybe he just fiddled with his keys."

"I can't understand what they get out of giving us a thousand dollars."

Amanda picked up her phone to google the man. Washingtongroupfund.com seemed too opaque; probably fraudulent. The phone had nothing to offer her. Her daughter was asleep down the hall! "Also, he looks familiar to me. Like, really."

"Well, I've never seen him before."

"You're terrible with faces." Clay never recognized the children's teachers and often accidentally passed long-standing neighbors on the street without acknowledging them. She knew he liked to think this implied that he was lost in thought, when really he was merely inattentive. "I don't believe this bullshit about the emergency broadcast system. We were just watching TV!"

"That's easy enough." Clay walked down the short hall. He pointed the remote control at the screen mounted on the wall. He'd half hoped (more than half) to broadcast some pornography there. It added a certain twist to things, but the technology was hard for him to parse—you had to get the television and the computer to cooperate. The television lit up. The screen was that blank digital blue. "That's weird."

"Is it on the right channel?"

"I was watching this morning. I think it's out."

"But it's not the emergency broadcast system. The satellite is probably out. It's probably the wind." Amanda was not going to be persuaded, because she could sense those people trying to persuade them. There was dishonesty in it.

"Fine, it's a glitch. But they said they heard that on the radio. The one doesn't mean the other isn't true."

"Why are you working so hard to believe everyone but your own wife?"

"I'm only trying to calm you down. I'm not saying I don't believe you, but . . ." He hesitated. He didn't believe her.

"There's something happening." Wasn't this the plot of *Six Degrees of Separation*? They let those people in because they were black. It was a way of acknowledging that they didn't believe all black people were criminals. A canny black criminal could take advantage of that!

"Or they're scared old people who need a place to stay tonight. We'll send them away in the morning."

"I'll never be able to sleep with strangers in the house!"

"Come on." Clay did wonder. Maybe the thousand dollars was a ruse, or there was something worth more than that in the house. He couldn't think straight.

"I think I've seen him before, I'm telling you." Amanda felt that frustration of being unable to recall a specific word. What if this was a revenge killing? He was some man she'd slighted years ago.

Clay knew that he was not good with faces. And he knew that maybe, on some level, he was especially not good with black faces. He wasn't going to say "They all look the same to me," but there was some evidence, actual biological, scientific evidence, that people were more adept at recognizing people of the same race. Like, it wasn't racist, was it, to admit that one billion Chinese probably looked more like one another to him than they did to one another. "I don't think we know him, and I don't think he's going to murder us." There was now some sliver, needle-sharp, of doubt. "I think we need to let them stay. It's the right thing to do."

"I want to see the proof." There was no way that she could make such a demand. "I mean, we have keys too! Maybe they rented it before us."

"This is their vacation house. It won't be on their license. I'll talk to them. If I get a bad feeling, we'll say, no, sorry, we're not comfortable with this arrangement. But if I don't, I think we let them stay. They're *old*."

"I wish I had your faith in other people." Amanda did not in fact envy Clay this trait.

"It's the right thing to do." Clay knew this would work; his wife felt it important, not to do the moral thing, necessarily, but to be the kind of person who would. Morality was vanity, in the end.

Amanda crossed her arms against her chest. She was right, in that she didn't know the whole story, nor did Clay, nor did the people in the kitchen, nor did the junior editor who, seeing the news cross the wire, issued the alert to the millions of people who had the *New York Times* app installed on their phones. The wind was so fierce, but even if it hadn't been, they likely would have been just too far from the flight path to hear the first planes dispatched to the coast, per protocol in that situation.

"We're going to be Good Samaritans." Clay turned the television off and stood, choosing in that moment not to mention the thousand dollars.

11

That day's morning seemed distant, like a story about someone else Clay had once been told. He could almost see the beach towels, drying on the railing outside, and they were like the pinch you're supposed to administer when you think you're dreaming. Amanda followed just behind him, and they came into the kitchen and found these strangers there, moving around like they owned the place, which, perhaps, they did.

"I made drinks. Felt like it was in order." G. H. gestured at the glass in his hand. "Our private reserve. I'm happy to get you one."

The man had left a cabinet ajar, and Clay could see inside of it bottles of Oban, wine, that expensive tequila in the porcelain vessel. He had done an inventory of the kitchen. Had he missed this, or had it been locked? "You know, I might have a drink."

G. H. poured one. "Ice? No ice?"

Clay shook his head and took the glass being offered. He sat at the island. "That's lovely, thank you."

"It's the least we can do!" The man gave a mirthless laugh.

There was a temporary silence, as though they'd planned it to memorialize someone now gone.

"I might need to excuse myself," Ruth said.

"Of course." Clay didn't know what was required of him. She wasn't asking his permission, and it wasn't his to grant.

Amanda watched the woman leave the room. She poured herself a glass of the wine she'd opened earlier because she wasn't sure what else to do. Her wine, the wine she'd paid for. She sat beside her husband. "It is a beautiful house." What a thing, to make small talk now.

G. H. nodded. "We love it. I'm happy to hear you do too."

"Have you been here long?" Amanda was trying to interrogate, hoping to catch him.

"Bought it five years ago now. We spent quite a while on the renovations, almost two years. But at this point it's home. Or home away from home."

"Whereabouts do you live in the city?" Clay knew how to make small talk too.

"We're on Park, between Eighty-First and Eighty-Second. What about you?"

Clay was cowed. The Upper East Side was uncool, but still holy. Or maybe so uncool that it was in fact cool. They'd held on to their place so long he could no longer comprehend real estate, the local sport. Still, he'd been in apartments on Park, upper Fifth, Madison. It always felt unreal, like a Woody Allen film. "We live in Brooklyn. Carroll Gardens."

"It's really Cobble Hill," Amanda said. She thought that more respectable. A better riposte to his uptown address.

"That's where everyone wants to live now, I guess. Younger people. I imagine you have more space than we do."

"Well, you have all this space here, in the country," Amanda said, reminding him of what she thought was his cover story.

"A big part of the reason we bought out here. Weekends, holidays. Get out of the city and into the fresh air. It's so different out here, the air."

"I like what you all did." Amanda stroked the countertop like it was a pet.

"We had a great contractor. So many of the little things were his idea."

Returning from the bathroom, Ruth paused in the living room to switch on the television. The screen was that vintage shade of blue from some simpler technological era, white letters important: emergency broadcast system. There was a beep, then a quiet hiss, the sound of something that was not much of a sound, then another beep. They kept coming, the beeps. There was nothing but the beeps, steady but not reassuring. The three others walked into the living room to see it for themselves.

"So, no news there," Ruth said, mostly to herself.

"It's probably just a test of the emergency broadcast system." Amanda was skeptical.

"It would say so if it was," Ruth said. It was common sense. "You see this."

They all saw it.

"Change the channel." Clay had faith. "We were just watching a show!"

Ruth scrolled through every available channel: 101, 102, 103, 104. Then more quickly: 114, 116, 122, 145, 201. All blues, those meaningless words. "This is some emergency broadcast system we've got."

"I'm sure it's nothing." Clay looked at the built-in shelves with remaindered art books and old board games. "It would tell us more if there were more to tell." Ipso facto.

"The satellite television is so unreliable. But it's impossible to get them to run the cable out this far, so it's the only option." Ruth had wanted the house to be far from everything. She'd been the one who wrote that Airbnb listing, and she meant it. That the house was a place apart from the rest of the world was the best thing about it.

"The wind is enough to knock it out." G. H. sat in one of the armchairs. "Rain. It's not very reassuring, that rain can affect a satellite. But it's true."

Clay shrugged his shoulders. "So there's an emergency. The emergency is that New York City is without power. But we still have it, even if we don't have TV or the internet. So that's got to make you feel better, I'd imagine? You were right to get out of the city—it must be a mess."

Amanda didn't believe this, but she also wondered. Should they fill the bathtub with water? Should they find batteries, candles, supplies?

"I think you should stay here tonight." Clay had seen enough evidence. "Tomorrow we'll sort out what's happening."

Amanda had nothing to say about the emergency broadcast system.

"A blackout could be something. It could be a symptom of something bigger." Ruth had ninety minutes to work it out and wanted to say it. "It could be fallout. It could be terrorism. It could be a bomb."

"Let's not let our imaginations run away." Clay's mouth was sugary from the drink.

"A bomb?" Amanda was incredulous.

G. H. didn't like to ask, but he had to. "You know, I'm sorry to trouble you, but we didn't have dinner. Some cheese and crackers before the concert."

The party—was it a party now?—retreated to the kitchen. Clay took the leftover pasta, still in its pot, out of the refrigerator. He was suddenly aware how messy the room was, how thoroughly they'd made themselves sloppily at home. "Let's eat something." He said it like it was his idea. Professors learned that, taking the occasional insightful classroom comment and transforming it into fact.

Ruth noticed that the sink was full of dirty dishes. She pretended not to be disgusted. "A dirty bomb in Times Square? Or some coordinated effort at the power plants?" She had never thought of herself as imaginative, but now she was discovering a flair for it. It only sounded like paranoia if you were wrong. Think of what had been done and forgotten in their lifetimes—in the past decade alone.

"We shouldn't speculate." G. H. was reasonable.

Someone had left the tongs inside the pot. The metal was cold to the touch. Clay filled four bowls, microwaved them in turn. "Where are the power plants in New York City?" There was so much you never knew in life, even someone smart like he was. Clay found this marvelous or meaningful. "They must be in Queens, I guess. Or by the river?"

"Some guy blows up a suitcase in Times Square. His pals do the same thing at the power plants. Synchronized chaos. The ambulances couldn't even get through the streets, if all the lights were out. Do the hospitals even have generators?" Ruth accepted a bowl of pasta. She didn't know what else to do, so she ate. Also, she was hungry. The pasta was too warm, but good, and she was unsure why this was something she begrudged. "This is very kind of you."

Amanda slurped accidentally. She was suddenly ravenous. Sensual pleasures reminded you that you were alive. Also, drinking too much made her hungry. "It's nothing."

G. H. could feel the food working on his chemistry. "It is delicious, thank you."

"It's the salted butter." Amanda felt the need to explain because it was unclear whether she was guest or host. She liked clarity about the role she was meant to discharge. "That European kind, shaped like a cylinder. It's a very simple recipe." She thought chat might salve the discomfort. She was embarrassed to have served this to strangers. The meal was just an improvisation that had ended up part of her repertoire. She liked to imagine some future summer, at some other rental house, the children back from Harvard and Yale, requesting this special dish that reminded them of their sun-filled childhood. "On vacation, I like to keep it simple. Burgers. Pancakes. That kind of thing."

"I'll do the washing." Ruth thought restoring her kitchen to order might soothe. Also it was only polite.

"We're here now. We're grateful to you both. I feel so much better, having eaten. I think I might have another drink." G. H. refilled. It was a whisky old enough to vote. It was for special occasions, but surely this counted.

"I'll join you." Clay slid his glass toward the man. "You see, there's nothing to worry about here." *Tumbler* was somehow fitting; the glass was heavy and expensive and it kept him from tumbling to the floor.

These strangers didn't know him, so they didn't know that G. H. was not given to hyperbole. In the hour and a half drive his fear had doubled like resting dough. "Well, it was disturbing." He had what he wanted, but now he wanted this man and this woman to understand him. He could sense their suspicion.

Ruth was calmed by the suds, the yellow sponge, the lemon scent, the squeak of a clean, hot plate. The preceding ninety minutes she'd been both suspended and speeding—modern life had an uncanny tempo, one man was never meant for. Cars and planes made time travelers of all of us. She'd looked out at the black night and shivered. She'd put a hand on G. H.'s knee. She'd thought about this place, this house, solidly made and tastefully furnished, beautifully situated and absolutely safe but for the complication of these people in her kitchen. "That's an understatement."

"A blackout. Like Hurricane Sandy." Clay recalled unfounded reports of an explosion, Superfund sludge from the Gowanus spilling into the water supply, every sip a carcinogen. They were without power a day and a half. It had been a kind of charming emergency; hunker down with playing cards and books. When the lights came back on, he had baked an apple pie.

"Or in 2003," Amanda said. "The electrical grid, remember that?"

"I walked across the Manhattan Bridge. Couldn't reach her on the phone." Clay put a hand on his wife's, nostalgic and possessive. "I was so worried. Of course, we were all remembering 9/11, but it was so much better than that day." That parochial one-upmanship New Yorkers think their own, special remit, but everyone is possessive of the places they inhabit. You recount the disasters to demonstrate your fidelity. You've seen the old girl at her worst.

"I thought of 9/11, of course." Ruth washed the food scraps down the drain and switched on the disposal. "What if people are dying right now? Remember a few years ago, that guy drove his truck on the bike path on the West Side? Just rented a truck in New Jersey and killed all those people? It's not even *difficult*. Like how much planning could that have possibly taken?"

"The lights. All the lights—" G. H. knew that no one was interested in hearing about the dream you had last night. This had been real, but maybe some things you had to see for yourself.

Clay believed if you said it, it would be true. "I think in the morning—"

"It *is* morning, now." Ruth met Clay's eyes in the reflection of the window, a neat little trick.

"I guess what I mean is that things always look different in the light of day. I guess self-help clichés are rooted in truth." Clay sounded apologetic, but he believed it. The world was not as fearful as people thought.

"I don't know how to explain it." Ruth dried her hands on a towel and hung it back where it belonged. A building lit up was alive, a beacon; dark, it vanished, like David Copperfield had made the Statue of Liberty do that one time. Ruth associated the sudden absence of light with something being extinguished, with a switch being flipped, with a change, and this invited the question: What had been extinguished, what switch flipped, what had changed?

"You've had a scare." Clay understood.

Ruth had learned only one thing from the current reality, and it was that everything held together by tacit agreement that it would. All it took to unravel something was one party deciding to do just that. There was no real structure to prevent chaos, there was only a collective faith in order. "I was scared. I am." This last part she didn't quite whisper. She wasn't ashamed, but she was embarrassed. Was this it, then; was she a fearful old woman now?

"We'll find out more tomorrow." Clay believed this.

"What if it's the North Koreans? That fat one who fed his own uncle to the dogs." Ruth could not stop herself. "What if it's a bomb. A missile." A year ago, was it, there was that false alarm in Hawaii where, for some terrible stretch, vacationers and honeymooners and dropouts and housewives and surf instructors and museum curators thought that was it, a missile was on its way from the Korean peninsula to obliterate them. How would you spend the last thirty-two minutes: looking for a basement or texting your friends or reading a story to your children or in bed with your spouse? People would probably monitor their own destruction by CNN play-by-play. Or the local stations wouldn't cut away, and you could go out watching *The Price Is Right*.

"The North Koreans?" Amanda said it like she'd never heard of the place. What if it was the Outer Mongolians? The Liechtensteiners? The Burkinabé? Did they even have the bomb in Africa? She'd watched Lorin Maazel conducting in Pyongyang. Some cable correspondent had promised détente, some previous president had promised them all peace. Amanda didn't have time to think about the North Koreans, and had no idea, even, what Ruth was talking about, feeding people to dogs; she thought the rap on the Koreans was that they were the ones who ate dogs.

"It's not the North Koreans." G. H. shook his head, but this was as remonstrative as he was willing to get. You didn't scold Ruth. She was a Barnard girl: she had ready answers. He fiddled with the heavy watch on his wrist, a nervous tic he knew was a tic. He had his money on Iran, maybe Putin. Not literally so; that was against the law. But he was no fool.

"How do you know?" Now that they were safe—but there was a question mark there—Ruth could cede to the panic that had been in her throat as they drove. She could say what she'd been unable to in the car, afraid of jinxing them with an empty tank or a punctured tire. She kept her silence and pictured the faces of her daughter and grandsons, the atheist's prayer. Muslim fundamentalists! Chechen true believers! Rebels in Colombia, Spain, Ireland, every country had its madmen.

"Wouldn't there have been a boom?" This was a familiar feeling for Clay, whenever he had to assemble furniture or the car made funny noises: how little he *knew*. Perhaps that was why, in his estimation, true intelligence was accepting how limited one's intelligence always is. This philosophy let him off the hook. "You would have . . . *heard* something. Like if it had been a bomb."

"I was having breakfast at Balthazar on 9/11." G. H. remembered the silky omelet, the salty French fries. "Can't be more than twenty blocks from the towers, right? I didn't hear a goddamn thing."

"Can we please not talk about 9/11?" Amanda was uncomfortable.

"I heard the sirens, and then people in the restaurant started talking, so—"

Ruth idly rapped her fingers against the countertop. There was no way to explain that the thing about dark is that it's rare. There's always some ambient light. There's always that contrast that helps you understand: *This is dark*. The pricks of stars, the leak beneath the door, the glow of an appliance, something. Wasn't its ability to assert itself, and at breakneck speed at that, light's most remarkable quality?

Without thinking, Clay gave his phone his fingerprint. The phone showed him a photograph of the children, Archie, then eleven, Rose, only eight, rounded, small, innocent. It was startling to look at this evidence of the selves now gone, though he often didn't truly see this picture, obscured by little squares of information, the seductive glow of the phone itself. He felt phantom tingles when the phone was not at his side. Clay recalled that in January, in the spirit of resolution, he'd tried leaving his phone in another room while he slept. But that was how he did most of his newspaper reading, and staying informed was as worthy a resolution. "Still nothing," he said, answering a question they all wanted to ask, even if none of them had bothered to. They decided to go to bed.

12

They had finished the basement for Ruth's mother, a dignified, withered creature, silk scarves and color-coordinated suits. She'd come to live with them when she turned ninety—much complaining, but the winters in Chicago were terrible, and there was no one left there to keep a close watch on her. Ruth had handled the sale of the house, sent disbursements to her sister and their brother, then moved Mama into the guest room. She liked to walk to the Met, look at the Impressionist paintings, then sit at the diner with a cup of tea and a Manhattan clam chowder. Had she not died, she'd be stranded in the dark three-bedroom on the fourteenth floor. Small mercy.

G. H. led the way downstairs, where they almost never went—that city dweller's fantasy: rooms you barely need—switching on the lights as he went. He had not realized how much light connoted safety, and how much dark its opposite. Even as a boy he'd not feared the dark, so this was a surprise. "Just watch your step," he said, some tenderness for his wife.

"This is my house." Ruth was holding tight to the railing. She felt it important to underscore this fact.

"Well, they paid for it." G. H. had driven fast, but there were some things that couldn't be outrun. His reticence was because of a very particular burden: he knew that something was wrong, truly wrong. "I can't exactly throw them out." G. H. didn't want to say that he had known something was coming. His business was clairvoyance. You looked at the yield curve arching and slumping like an inchworm making its inefficient progress, and it told you everything you needed to know. He had known not to trust that particular parabola. It was more than portent, it was a promise. Something was upon them. It had been decreed.

"You saw how dirty they had the kitchen." Ruth didn't need to say *What would Mom think of that?* because Mom hovered around. The basement had been intended for her—an exterior ramp around the back of the house, easier than the stairs—but she died before she got to visit. Ruth knew she was evolving into a pale imitation of the woman. Another way of saying she was old. It just happened. You found yourself holding your grandbabies—twins!—and not saying anything about the fact that they had two moms. Clara was a professor of classics at Mount Holyoke. Maya was the headmaster of a Montessori school. They had a big, cold clapboard house with a turret. Mom would have got a kick out of her mocha-colored great-grandsons, made of the genetic issue of Clara's brother, James, who did something in Silicon Valley. The boys looked just like both of their mothers, something you'd not have thought possible, but there it was, in black and white, ha ha ha.

G. H. flicked on lights, forgetting to pause in gratitude that they still worked. There was a big closet: a cache of Duracells, a flat of Volvic, some bags of Rancho Gordo beans, boxes of Clif Bars and Barilla fusilli stored in a heavy-duty plastic bin because there were mice in the country. Cans of tuna, a gasoline canister's worth of olive oil, a case of a cheap Malbec that was not half bad, bed linens in those vacuum bags that sucked out all the air. The two of them could be comfortably housebound for a month, if not longer. G. H. practically dared a snowstorm to arrive, but thus far none had. They said that was global warming. "Everything in order."

She murmured something to show she heard him. They'd spent too much remodeling. Improvement was an addiction. G. H.'s business was money's preservation. Actual spending was so abstract to him that he did as the contractor said. Danny was one of those men other men didn't want to seem a fool in front of. He had a power over men that was almost sexual, in the way that sex always ends up being about power. You'd do what he said, and maybe in your worst moments you'd worry that Danny was laughing at you. Their checks had certainly paid for Danny's daughter's year at private school. That's why they rented: to recoup.

"It smells down here." Ruth made a face, but it didn't really smell. Rosa cleaned the place, her husband tended the lawn, and their kids came out and assisted. It was a family affair. They were from Honduras. Rosa would not have left a smell. The carpet's nap said that she vacuumed even the unused basement. There was a bedroom, with a sofa and a table and a wall-mounted television, the bed made up and expectant. She sat and slipped off her shoes.

"It doesn't." G. H. sat on the edge of the bed, more heavily than he meant to. He couldn't stop himself sighing when he did things like that. He tried to imagine the morning's relief. The funny news on the radio—a band of raccoons broke into a substation in Delaware and knocked out power all over the East Coast, or some subcontractor's most junior employee had a terrible first day. What were we worried about, what were we afraid of? Market confidence would be restored; there would be a windfall for certain stoic bettors.

Ruth was at a loss. Their normal routine was to first unlock all the cabinets filled with their special and necessary things: swimsuits and flip-flops, Shiseido sunscreen, a wool Hermès picnic blanket, and in the pantry, a tin of Maldon salt, a bottle of olive oil from Eataly, the horrifyingly sharp Wusthof knives, four jars of Luxardo cherries, Clase Azul, Oban, Hendrick's, the wines guests had brought as hostess gifts, dry vermouth, bitters. They'd reunite with those possessions: rub them on their skin, scatter them around the rooms, and feel truly at home. They'd pull off their clothes—what was the point having a home in the country if you couldn't walk around mostly naked?—and make Manhattans and slip into the pool or the hot tub or just into the bed. They still went to bed with each other, aided by those most effective blue tablets. "I'm scared."

"We're here." He paused because it was important to remember. "It's safe here." He thought of his canned tomatoes. There was enough to last them for months.

There were unopened toothbrushes in the bathroom drawer. There were fresh towels, rolled jauntily and stacked in a little pyramid. Ruth showered. Feeling clean made such a difference to her. In the bedroom dresser there was an old T-shirt from a charity run she couldn't remember, a pair of shorts she could not identify. She put these on, felt immediately ridiculous. She didn't want the people upstairs to see her in these cheap clothes.

G. H. tried the bedroom television, because he was curious. It showed nothing, just a blue screen, channel after channel. He undid his tie. When she'd been alive, G. H. had felt Mom's presence as an indictment. G. H. was so accustomed to being who he was and had come to believe that was success. When Mom had come out to inspect Maya, she'd rebuked him for his fourteen-hour days, for living so high up (unnatural!), for the delusion of their New York lives. It had shaken him. They changed their lives. They bought the place on Park, sent Maya to Dalton, and lived prudently. Sometimes he did miss the ground underfoot. The wisdom of the elders.

Ruth returned in a billow of steam.

"I tried the television. Same thing." He had to share this with her, though he had not expected otherwise.

She shifted and adjusted under the clean bedding. The wind was noisy. "So, what do you think it is?" She didn't want to be humored.

G. H. knew her. It had been decades! "I think it's

something we're going to laugh about when we hear what it was. That's what I think." He didn't think this. But it was right to lie sometimes. He looked at himself in the mirror and thought about their apartment, their home, the suits in his walk-in closet, the coffee maker he'd settled on after spending weeks researching. He thought about the planes over Manhattan and how it must have looked to their passengers as the place went dark. He thought about the satellites over the planes over Manhattan and the pictures they were taking and what they would show. He thought about the space station over the satellites over the planes and wondered what the multiracial, multinational crew of scientists would have made of the whole thing from their unique vantage. Sometimes distance showed a thing most clearly.

G. H. understood electricity as a commodity. This wasn't some vicissitude in the market. You couldn't pull the plug on the nation's financial capital. Insurance companies would be in litigation for decades. If the lights went out in New York City, that was act-of-God stuff. Act of God. The kind of thing his mother-in-law might have said.

13

Your kid's voice could wake you up, your kid's presence could wake you up. Amanda felt Rose's fat little body rock into the gulf between her and Clay even before she felt the girl's wet breath too near her ear.

"Mom, Mom." A soft hand on her arm, gentle but also insistent.

She sat up. "Rosie." The previous year the girl had declared she was done with the *ie*. "Rose."

"Mom." Rose was wide awake. Rose restored by the night. Rose, abloom. It had been this way her whole life. Mornings, she was dying to *do*. She opened her eyes and jumped to the floor. (Mrs. Weston, the neighbor downstairs, had raised two daughters in the same eleven hundred square feet, so she never complained.) Rose didn't understand how her brother could stay asleep until eleven, twelve, one. Mornings, everything seemed thrilling to her—wash face, choose clothes, read a book. Rose was enthusiastic. Everything was possible. When you're the younger child, you learn to fend for yourself. "There's something wrong with the TV."

"Honey, this is not an emergency." Then she remembered: *This is the emergency broadcast system.* Amanda slapped the too-slack pillows into obeisance.

"It's all messed up." The first few channels were black and white, dancing light. After that, all white, just nothing.

They'd forgotten to draw the blinds. Outside it was light, but indirect. Not clouds but the early hour. The storm they'd thought was coming wasn't after all. As she looked at it, the squat clock bedside ticked from 7:48 to 7:49. So: electricity. Some blackout. "Honey. I don't know."

"Can't you fix it?" Rose was just young enough to believe her parents could do anything. "It's not fair, it's a vacation, and you said on vacation we can watch as much television or have as much screen time as we want."

"Daddy's sleeping. Go wait in the living room, I'm coming."

Rose stomped away—that was how she walked—

and Amanda picked up her phone. The screen woke up, happy to see her, and she was happy, too: not one news alert but four. But just as before, she couldn't see more than the dispatch. She pressed on the alert and the screen tried and failed to connect. The same headline—"Major Blackout Reported on the East Coast of the United States"—then "Hurricane Farrah Makes Landfall in North Carolina"—then "Breaking: East Coast of the United States Reports Power Failure"— then a final "Breaking" followed by nonsensical letters. She hoped the television would work. But they'd stopped listening to NPR when four-year-old Rosie had intoned "I'm David Greene," and seven-year-old Archie asked about Pussy Riot. They'd protected the kids from so much.

Amanda smoothed the sheet under her hand, bumped Clay's ass. "Clay." He mumbled, and she shook him by the shoulder. "Get up. Look."

His mouth was sour, eyes unfocused. Amanda had her phone in his face. He made an unintelligible sound.

"Look." She shook the phone again.

"I can't see." In those moments of waking, it was impossible to see anything. You had to force your eyes to focus. But really he meant the phone had gone dark. She jabbed at it. "Oh, here."

"What?" He remembered last night, but could not push himself from sleep into wakefulness so quickly. "It looks like no one murdered us."

She ignored this. "The news."

The screen before him said nothing. "Amanda, it doesn't say anything." Just the date, just the same photograph, a snapshot of the kids they'd used as their Christmas card two years before.

"It was just there." She needed Clay to share the burden of this information.

He yawned; it went on for a long moment. "Are you sure? What did it say?"

"Of course I'm sure." Was she? Amanda studied the phone. "How do you see the alerts? It's not opening the app. But there were four. That same one about the blackout, then another one about the blackout, and something about that hurricane, and one that just said 'breaking,' and it was—"

"Breaking what?"

"It just said a bunch of gibberish."

"They abuse that 'breaking.' Breaking, polls show the Liberal Democrats take the lead in the Austrian congressional races. Breaking, Adam Sandler says his new movie is his best work yet. Breaking, Doris Who Gives a Fuck, inventor of the automatic ice cream maker, dead at age ninety-nine."

"No, like it was. Not even words. Just letters. It must have been a mistake."

"Maybe that's the network. The cell network? Maybe there's something wrong with that? Would a blackout affect that?" Clay didn't know how the world fit together. Who truly did, though?

"You think there's something wrong with the cell phones? Or is it just where we are? Because my phone's been spotty since we got here. It worked in town, when I went to the grocery."

"We are sort of far away. This happened last year, too, remember? And that place we rented wasn't nearly as remote."

Or, she didn't say, something so bad happened that even the *New York Times* was affected. Amanda stood and drank from the bottle on the bedside. It was room temperature, and what she most wanted was cold water. "Four news alerts. I didn't even get that many on election night." She went to the bathroom, studied the phone as she peed. It did not tell her any more.

Clay pulled on the boxer shorts he'd lost in the night and looked out at the backyard. Despite the portent of storm, it seemed like any other summer morning. Even the wind seemed to have abated. Indeed, had he looked—closer than it was possible for him to look— he'd have understood the stillness as a response to that wind. He'd have noticed that the insects had gone quiet; he'd have noticed that the birds were not calling. Had he noticed, he'd have noted that it was like those strange moments when the moon passed before the sun, that temporary shadow the animals did not understand.

She left the bathroom and passed her husband waiting for his turn. "I'll make some coffee." The phone felt heavy in her thin cotton pocket.

Rose was at the kitchen island with a bowl of cereal. Amanda remembered (it was not so long ago) when the girl had needed adult intercession to fetch the bowl, fill it, slice the banana, pour the milk. She had tried not to resent it at the time; she had tried to remember how fleeting those days were. And now they were gone. There was a last time that she had sung the children to sleep, a last time she had wiped the feces from the recesses of their bodies, a last time she had seen her son nude and perfect as he was the day she met him. You never know when a time is the last time, because if you did you could never go on with life. "Hi, baby." She scooped dry coffee into the paper filter. Another normal, beautiful day, right?

"Can I watch a movie on your computer?"

"The internet is out, honey, otherwise I'd let you watch Netflix. Listen. I have to tell you—"

"This vacation sucks." Rose had a point to make. Injustice.

"—last night, these people—the Washingtons—the people who own this house, they had to come by, there's been—" What noun did she need? "There was a problem. With their car. And they were not far from here, so they came here, even though they rented the house to us for the week." You had to be willing to lie, to be a mother or maybe just a person. Sometimes you had to lie.

"What are you talking about?" Rose already didn't care. She wanted to text Hazel and see what she was doing. Hazel was probably watching television right that very minute.

"There was a problem with the car and they weren't far away and they knew we were here, but they thought maybe they could just come and explain and—" It was not even hard to dissemble. The children couldn't hold complex things—even simple things, really—in their heads, and also they didn't care, beautiful narcissists.

Clay in his boxer shorts and sleepy eyes. "I'll take some of that coffee."

Amanda filled a mug. "I was just telling Rose about the Washingtons."

"Dad, the TV isn't working." Rose tugged on his

arm. He was the one who would care. He was the one who would help her.

The hot liquid splashed onto his right foot. "Easy, baby."

"Did you forget to put your bowl in the sink?" Amanda had read a book on how to talk so kids will listen. "Clay, you should put clothes on. Those people are here." She heard the rudeness in this. "The Washingtons. They're just downstairs."

"Dad, can you fix it?"

"Let's just slow it down." Maybe they'd been too permissive about screen time, parceled out like the narcotic that it was. Clay was unable to resist her entreaties. As a toddler, she'd called for Daddy in a way that was very specific. A girl needed her father. He put his coffee down and fiddled with the remote control. Snow, a bit of poetry for what you saw when the signal was broken. "Yeah. This doesn't look like it's working."

"Can't you, like—reset it or something? Or go up onto the roof or whatever?"

"No one is going on the roof," Amanda said.

"I'm not going on the roof." He scratched at his belly, stippled with hair, swollen from midnight pasta. "Besides, I'm not even sure if the problem is here, on the roof, or—somewhere else." His gesture indicated everything around them. Who could answer for the world at large? Was it even . . . still there? "Why don't you go sit outside. I'll come join you—I just need to talk to Mom for a second."

Rose would have preferred television, but also she just needed a task. She would accept her father's attention. "You're coming."

"Just give me two minutes." He looked past her at the morning, pale yellow and reluctant.

She said "Fine" the way adolescents learn to pronounce it, with all the fervor of any four-letter word. The morning was quiet. It was pretty, but not as interesting as a television show.

Rose slammed the door behind her without entirely meaning to. It was definitely nicer wherever Hazel was. Her television would never not work. Her parents let her have an unlocked Instagram account. Rose sat on one of the white metal chairs and looked at the woods.

Where the yard shrugged away from the house, the grass grew patchy and was then just dust and leaves and weeds at the hem of the woods or wilderness or whatever it was. In the space beyond that, Rose saw a deer, with abbreviated velvet antlers and a cautious yet somehow also bored mien, considering her through dark, strangely human eyes.

She wanted to say "A deer," but there was no one there to hear her. She looked over her shoulder into the house and saw her parents talking. She wasn't supposed to go in the pool, but she wasn't going to go in the pool. She walked down the steps onto the damp grass and the deer just watched her, barely curious. She hadn't even seen that there was another beside it—no more. There were five deer, there were seven; every time Rose adjusted her eyes to try to understand what she was seeing, she was seeing something new. There were dozens of deer. Had she been up higher, she'd have understood that there were hundreds, more than a thousand, more than that, even. She wanted to run inside and tell her parents, but she also wanted to just stand there and see it.

14

Ruth woke with lucid eyes and sudden memory. That familiar sensation of jerking awake when you're falling asleep, something you take for private idiosyncrasy then learn is part of the human condition. The quotidian sounds of morning: water in pipes, someone else's footsteps, a conversation from another room. She was desperate for Maya. She was in bed but also still in the car, thinking of the girl: baby at her breast, toddler on her lap, ten with thick limbs and box braids, terse teen in flannel shirt and too many earrings, college girl, blushing wife, radiant mother. Every version of Maya overlapped in Ruth's mind. The green light on the cable box showed her that the power still flowed. Her cell phone still did not seem to reach the world, but she hadn't expected it to. She let George sleep, crept upstairs.

In the kitchen, Ruth picked up the telephone Danny had suggested installing. The contractor had some kind of hold over George. Men of G. H.'s generation didn't think of affection for other men. That had made it the more charming and then annoying to watch G. H. fall under Danny's spell. The man was a manual laborer; G. H. had gone to Harvard Business School. But Danny was muscled and capable in his chambray shirts, sleeves rolled over firm forearms, sunglasses perched on the back of his head. She pressed the receiver against her ear. Not the steady basso of a phone ready to be dialed; the dirge that told you the thing was already dead. For a terrible moment Ruth couldn't quite imagine the sound of her daughter's voice. What did Maya, today's Maya, the real person, sound like?

As an adult, she was the same as she'd been as a child, mostly bemused by her parents. She favored long, strange dresses in a riot of colors and patterns. Her children were called Beckett and Otto and toddled around on the back lawn naked. Ruth didn't understand their names or the fact that they had foreskins, but she kept this to herself. She put the phone down, too forceful, maybe.

The couple were in the living room. The man was barely dressed, the woman in her comfortable clothes.

Amanda tried not to show that she was startled. "Good morning."

Ruth returned this pleasantry, as was normal. It was insincere or inaccurate, or perhaps both. "The telephone is still out."

"We were just— Amanda had alerts on her phone this morning."

"What did they say?" Ruth wondered why her phone had told her nothing. She never could quite master the damn thing.

"The same thing, a blackout. Then something about that hurricane. Then an update, then something that was just gibberish." This was the third time she'd explained it; the information felt even more meaningless now.

"Let me get you some coffee," Clay said. He felt embarrassed, undressed.

"A hurricane. That's something." Ruth tried to make it mean something.

"Is it?" Clay handed her a mug (her mug).

"Well, yes, maybe it's related. To the power outage. That could be. There was Hurricane Sandy, of course. I don't remember hearing that this one was bound for New York, but I wasn't paying close attention, I have to admit." They'd all heard, she knew, that those storms of the century were going to be storms of the decade. That there might have to be a new category introduced to accurately describe the kinds of storms, now that humankind had so altered the ocean.

"I'm not sure what to tell the kids." Amanda looked at the stranger as though she might have some advice, then turned toward the French doors, and they all did, all looked at Rose, standing down in the yard.

"How old is she?" Years ago, Ruth was asked to help out in the school office. Dalton wanted to increase *diversity*. Now Ruth was immune to kids' germs and mostly impervious to their charms.

"Just thirteen. Last month." Amanda was protective. "But still kind of a baby at heart. So I would love to keep . . . things between the adults."

"There's no need to worry them." At school, Ruth treated kids as the selves they'd inevitably be. The boys who would turn out handsome and therefore catered to, the girls who would turn out pretty and therefore cruel, the rich ones who would become Republicans, the rich ones who would become drug addicts, the rich ones who would exceed their parents' expectations of them, the poor ones who would prosper and the poor ones who would skulk from Princeton back to East New York. She knew that childhood was a temporary condition. But being a grandmother had made her soft.

"I don't want the kids to panic over nothing." Amanda tried not to imply that this was what Ruth and her husband had done.

Ruth's mother would have invoked God. Life was about making sure your children do better than you did, and Ruth's atheism was a definite improvement. You can't get through life dismissing the incomprehensible as divine. "I don't want to scare anyone." But she was afraid. "Thank you for the coffee."

"We have—there are eggs, cereal, you know." Clay held a banana, not knowing how like a primate he looked in that moment. "I'm going to go get dressed," he said, quite forgetting his promise to his daughter. He had a plan.

Ruth sat. She felt safe in small talk. "So. What is it you do?"

This Amanda understood. "I'm in advertising. On the client side. Manage relationships." She sat, too, crossed one leg over the other.

Ruth took her turn. "I'm retired now. I was in admissions. At the Dalton school."

Amanda couldn't help sit up a little straighter. Perhaps there was an angle. Her children, not exceptional (still wonderful in her estimation!), could do with an advantage. She knew the tuition was a suggestion. Families like theirs relied on the largesse of luckier people. "That's so interesting."

From her old office Ruth sometimes saw Woody Allen, poking around in the house directly opposite. That was one of three or four interesting things about it. She was happy to be free. "And your husband?"

"Clay? He's a professor. English, but also media studies."

"I'm not sure I know what that means." She said it like a little joke on herself.

Amanda was never entirely clear on it either. "Films. Literacy. The internet. The truth, that kind of thing."

"At Columbia?"

"City College." It seemed like a disappointment, since the woman's first guess had been the Ivy but Amanda was proud.

"I was at Barnard. Then Teachers College." Ruth was doing this routine because she wanted to understand these people a little better. It was a give-and-take.

"A true New Yorker. I went to Penn. Philadelphia seemed so urban to me. So exotic." She remembered driving onto campus, her parents' Corolla bursting with jersey sheets, desk lamp, shower caddy, Tori Amos poster. The place had looked flat. She heard "city" and had been picturing buildings reaching for the sky. Still, it was better than Rockville. REM was right: nobody says hello, don't talk to anybody they don't know. "I wish I'd gone to college in New York."

"Well, I'm from Chicago." Ruth said it like it was the best place to be from. "But I suppose I'm a true New Yorker now. More years there than not."

G. H. had dressed—skipping the dirty underwear and sweat-in socks, not bothering with the tie—and made up the bed. Not making up the bed was no kind of life. He had tried to prepare himself, the usual ablutions, but was vague about what he was preparing himself for. "Good morning."

Amanda stood to greet him, some formality she did not know was her nature.

"Any news?" He listened to Amanda's report of what they barely knew and wished he could see the news, but he also wished he could see the market. He wanted information but also vindication. "The storm, I'm sure. A downed limb."

"The landlines *don't* go. That's the whole reason Danny said to put one in." Ruth didn't mind being mollified, but she did not want to be lied to.

"The power is still on." G. H. did not want this overlooked. "Maybe today we should drive over to

Danny's." If you were going to be under some kind of terrorist siege, you'd want to be with Danny.

"Who's Danny? Are there neighbors nearby? We passed that farm stand, just before the turn onto the lane. There must be someone there. Maybe they know something." Amanda did not know that the itch she felt was so like the one that afflicted her husband when he was too long without nicotine. She wanted away.

"What if. Collective hysteria. Groups of people get some malady that turns out to just be a shared delusion. Hundreds of people with tremors and fever, imagining a rash. They can even make their skin turn pink." G. H. was only offering a theory.

Ruth brought her husband a coffee. "You're going to call me hysterical—the word people, *men*, use for women." Cassandra had, of course, been right about Troy.

"We saw the same thing. Something happened, sure, I think we can agree." But this was a technicality, it was the nature of the world, things happening.

"You drove." She meant he ran. "You were as afraid as me."

"Well, the elevator." Their floor was termed the fourteenth, but it was not. The building lacked a thirteenth floor because that was terrible luck. Simply pretending it wasn't there was better.

Amanda felt embarrassed. She didn't know these people and couldn't watch them bicker. "Where does Danny live?"

"Not far. You can't do anything in life without the right information. I'll drive over there." G. H. looked out at the day. The morning looked odd to him, but he could not articulate why, could not be certain it was not context instead of fact.

"I don't want you going anywhere." Ruth scoffed at the idea of seeking refuge at Danny's, like he was their son instead of someone they paid. She was working through all the possible scenarios. Some Muslim with nothing to live for strapped into explosives. Another plane crash—why didn't those happen more? It was brilliant to turn a plane into a weapon.

The little house felt safe. Amanda understood.

"I need my clothes. I need clean clothes." Ruth looked toward Amanda.

"Oh. Of course."

"I just need to go into my closet." They rented the house, but they'd never actually seen strangers inside it. They always had Rosa in before they came out. They always found the house spotless and chilled and ready to receive them.

"Clay's just getting dressed, I'll ask him to hurry."

Ruth didn't need to say anything about the look

on their faces when they'd opened the door to them. Guess who's coming to dinner? "Thank you."

Ruth was sixty-three years old. She hadn't been raised to *do*—though that had been expected—but to convince. This was, her mother understood, how women made their way in the world: convincing men to do the things they wanted. "I'm scared." She was confessing. "Maya and the boys. She's probably trying to call us."

"Our daughter," G. H. explained. He put a hand on his wife's shoulder. "Don't worry about that now."

She mostly could bear not thinking about the ice caps or the president. She could hold fear at bay by focusing on the small matter of her own life. "You remember that year we went to Italy?"

Dry heat, a luxury hotel, Maya in her pigtails. They'd sipped glasses of sweet juice, they'd eaten pizza topped with rosemary and potatoes, they'd rented a car, they'd stayed in a villa in the country. It was a flat, near treeless place with the mercy of a swimming pool. Maya, taking in the rubble that was the Forum, asked why they'd come there to see a place so wholly wrecked. History meant nothing to her. Time was unimaginable at nine. Maybe it was at sixty-three too. There was only that moment, the current moment, this life. "What made you think of that?"

"I don't know what else to think about," Ruth said.

15

Rose turned the secret of the deer over and over, as you would a hard candy on your tongue. She was not yet old enough that her words would be believed. They would say she'd made it up. They would say she'd exaggerated. They would say she was a child. But Rose felt the change in the day, even if no one else did. For starters, it was hot, impossibly so, given the sun had not fully come up. The air felt artificial, like inside a greenhouse or some botanical garden exhibition. The morning was too quiet. It was telling her something. She tried to hear what.

In the kitchen, her father was talking to an old man she'd never seen. Rose did not bother reminding her father that he'd been supposed to come see her outside.

It was better that he had forgotten. He made introductions.

"Nice to meet you." Rose was well brought up.

"A pleasure." G. H. couldn't help think of his own daughter. He remembered he'd used her name for the combination to the lockbox.

"Did you brush your teeth?" Clay wanted to get rid of the girl.

"It's super hot outside. Can I swim?"

"Fine with me. Just find your mother first. Tell her I said it was okay. I need to talk to Mr. Washington."

In the night, somehow, each man had forgotten the other, would have been unable to describe him to a police sketch artist. They said eyewitnesses were unreliable anyway; most people cared only for themselves. That was true of both these men, rudderless without precedent for etiquette, in a house to which they each laid claim.

Seeing the man again, in the day's light, was like seeing a stranger with whom you'd had sex. "G. H., would you mind if we stepped outside?" This sounded so masculine and decisive if you didn't know that Clay wanted a cigarette.

"Let's do that." G. H. chuckled a little. It was hard not to assume the role of genial sitcom neighbor. Television created the context, and black people had to play along. But this was his house. He was the protagonist of his story.

They left through the side door. G. H. was proprietary about even the grounds. Thicket was right—the lawn petered out at a wall of trees. It was different than having a home at the sea. The ocean loomed. The trees were protective. "Hot out." He looked at the sky and noted how pale it was.

Clay produced cigarettes from his pocket. "A little vice—I'm sorry."

G. H. understood: man to man. Men didn't say such things anymore, they just implied them. Once it had been one of the secretary's responsibilities to empty the desktop ashtrays. Now you didn't even say "secretary" but "assistant." "I understand."

They walked past the hedgerow. The gravel crunched pleasantly underfoot. Clay went farther than necessary—the hedge obscured them, the children would not see—because he felt this was respectful. "I wouldn't smoke in the house, you know."

"There's a reason we ask for the security deposit." They'd had fine luck with renters. A broken wineglass, a loose doorknob, a missing soap dish that Ruth had replaced with a large seashell.

"Amanda told you what she saw? The news alerts."

These didn't worry him, only the one that was gibberish. He worried about the technology more than the nation.

G. H. nodded. "Do you know what I do for a living? I manage money. And do you know what you need to do that job? Information. That's it. Well, money. But information. You can't make choices, you can't assess risks, unless you know something."

But Clay wanted to be the one. Clay wanted to put everyone at ease. Clay was just selfish enough. "I'm going to drive into town. It's the only way."

"I suspect it's terrorism. But that's not what scares me. Terrorists are dumb hicks. That's how you convince them to incinerate themselves for God. They're patsies. But what comes next?" G. H. once had faith in the institutions of American life, but he had less now. "Let's say something happens in New York City. Do you think this president will do the right thing about it?" This kind of thing used to sound like paranoia, but now it was just pragmatism.

"Well, I'm going to get to the bottom of it." Clay was proud of himself. His chest swelled in some primate's instinct.

"My contractor lives just a few miles down the road. He's a good man. I trust him. We could head over there." G. H. was mostly thinking out loud.

Clay was relieved by the nicotine. "We're safe out here, I think."

G. H. was less certain. "It seems so. At the moment."

"I don't think we need to bother your friend. I'm going to go into town. Buy a newspaper. Find someone who knows more than we do."

"I'd say I'd join you, but I'm not sure if Ruth would approve." He was a dealmaker by trade. He didn't want to go.

"You stay here." Clay was thinking, on some level, of his father. "You see those rentals where the homeowner is on the premises. Hosts. It's really not so odd." He worried about them driving more. He thought this was decent of him. He wanted to be seen to be good.

G. H. looked again at the sky. "It looks like it might be a nice day. Very hot out already." When you got older you could say that kind of thing, as though you were somehow in tune with nature's secret rhythms, as though G. H. had spent his life on a fishing trawler instead of in a Midtown skyscraper. Maybe he'd have a swim.

Clay looked up too. The yellow was setting into blue. He'd thought it seemed like rain, but now it felt like summer. How wrong they'd been!

16

He pressed the button twice to lower all four windows simultaneously. Clay appreciated this feature, the brainstorm of one particularly insightful engineer who understood that on a hot day the first thing you wanted was air. There was, though, a kind of pleasure in the close dry heat inside the car, flecks of dust, the way you could almost smell the sunlight. The wheels made a particular noise on the gravel, then cleared that and moved smoothly over the asphalt. He drove slowly, nonchalant, to make himself feel the more brave. Also, he figured, the longer those people stayed, the more right he had to their thousand dollars.

There was a field of something being cultivated, but Clay had no idea what it was. Were soybeans the same thing as edamame, or were they something else, and what could they be used for? He drove slowly past the little shack selling eggs. The road was an intermediate thing, still narrow, not quite real; he waited for the GPS to register, but hadn't he found the way to the shore only yesterday morning? Clay knew what he was doing.

Someone had once told him that people found smoking calming because it was essentially deep breathing. There was no shoulder, so he simply stopped in the road, turned the machine off, depressed the button to bring the windows back up in beautiful unison. He stood ten feet away because he didn't want the smell of smoke to permeate the car.

There was that familiar, pure rush of satiety. There was an almost swoon. He had nothing to lean on, so he simply drew himself up taller and looked around at the world, which was quiet. He had a fleeting desire for the clarity of a cold Coke, to shake off the vague hangover. That's what he would do. He'd drive down this road, turn onto the main road, wind around the curves and end up at that four-way intersection and instead of bearing right, toward the sea, he'd go left, toward the town. There was a gas station, there was a public library, there was a junk shop and an ice cream parlor and a motel, and farther down the road one of those depressing low-lying complexes with a grocery, drugstore, dry cleaner, and chain sandwich shop tidily arrayed before a parking lot so large it would never fill up. That's where he'd go in search of knowledge, not to the library but to the place where things were sold. You could get a Coke almost anywhere.

Clay looked at his phone. Habit was powerful. It showed him nothing. He dropped the cigarette and stepped on it, then got back into the car. The brain was a marvel. You could drive without wholly thinking about driving. Sure, familiar routes, the everyday commute—start the car, find the highway, maneuver through lanes, take the usual exit, glide to stops at red lights, move forward at green ones—while not exactly hearing the top stories being reiterated on NPR, or thinking about some slight at the office, or remembering a production of *The Pirates of Penzance* you saw the summer between sixth and seventh grades. Driving was rote. It was something you just did.

He wasn't actually thinking about the production of *The Pirates of Penzance* he'd seen the summer between sixth and seventh grades, though he remembered that as the golden, temporary season in which he'd still been his mother's favorite child, but he must have been thinking about something because Clay turned, at some point, and drove for some distance—he found estimating distance and measures of volume impossible—and realized that though he was definitely on a road, a more serious, two-lane road, the sort of road the GPS would know and name, he could not be certain, not really, that it was the road he'd wanted. There were directions written down in Amanda's notebook, of course, but Amanda's notebook was back at the house, in Amanda's Vuitton bag. Anyway, the ability to take written directions to one destination and simply invert them to move in reverse was an obsolete art. It was like winding the car windows down with a crank. Human progress. Clay was lost.

Everything was very green. There was nothing to hold on to. There were some trees. There was a field. A glimpse of a roof and the promise of a building, but he couldn't say whether it was a barn or a house. The road curved, and then he emerged somewhere else where there was another field and some more trees and another slice of roof of barn or house and Clay thought of those old cartoons that recycled their backgrounds to create the illusion of movement. It was impossible to say what was more sensible—to stop the car and backtrack or to forge ahead as though he knew where he was going. He didn't even know how long he'd been driving, or whether he'd know the turn back onto the road that led to the gravel driveway up to the house where his family waited. He didn't know whether that road was marked by a sign or what the sign would say. Maybe he ought to have paid closer attention; maybe he ought to have taken this errand more seriously.

The sound of the wind and the sensation of it on his face was distracting. Clay slowed the car a little and sent the windows back up, then jabbed at the center panel until the air-conditioning came to life. He continued straight, but that wasn't exactly correct, since the road undulated and twisted and maybe he'd gone in a complete circuit and that was why the trees and occasional buildings looked so familiar: because they were. He found a piece of gum and put it in his mouth. Fine.

There were no other cars, and he didn't know if that seemed odd or not. Anyway, it was not the kind of road for stop signs. The local planners trusted the local people. He pulled onto the dusty shoulder and turned the car around and drove in the direction from which he'd come. Now nothing looked familiar, though he'd just driven through it. It was all inverted, and he noticed things on the left side of the road that he'd missed when they had been on his right: an amateurish painted sign reading "McKinnon Farms," a lone horse standing in a field, the remains of a building that had burned down. He drove and then slowed, because he felt he must be close to the turn back to the house. But he wouldn't take that, he would drive on in the other direction, where he knew the town waited.

There was a road on his right, and he turned to look up it as he passed, but it was not the road that led to the house, because that road had that little painted shack where you could get a dozen eggs for five dollars. He sped up and drove on. There was another turnoff, but again, no painted shack. Then he wondered whether he'd turned twice to get to the road where he now found himself, and was looking for a landmark that did not exist. Clay took out his phone, though he knew you weren't supposed to look at your phone as you drove, and was surprised that it did not seem to be working. Then he remembered that of course it had not been working, that was the real purpose of this errand, not an ice-cold Coke. He had driven out to show everyone that he was a man, in control, and now he was lost and felt ridiculous.

He tossed the phone into the seat beside him. Of course there were no other cars. These were rural roads, for the convenience of a handful of people. The day only seemed strange because the night had been strange. He was a little turned around, but he would find his way; he hadn't gone so far that he'd need rescue. He thought of how the government sent helicopters for the antisocial weirdos who insisted on living atop wildfire-prone mountains. People thought fire a disaster, failing to understand it was an important part of the life cycle of the forest. The old burned. The new grew. Clay kept driving. What else was he supposed to do?

17

The sun crept across the sky as ever it had. They welcomed it; they worshipped it. The prickle on the skin felt like punishment. The sweat felt like virtue. Cups collected on the table. Towels were used and abandoned. There were sighs and feints toward conversation. There was the plash of water and the sound of the door opening and closing. It was the kind of heat you could almost hear, and in that kind of heat what could you do but swim?

Amanda worried fresh sunscreen into her chest and could feel the stuff of herself, ropy and fibrous, beneath her skin. It was an improvisation. Someone in the audience's shadows had shouted out this scenario. It made no sense, and she was tasked with performing as though it did. Clay driving into town. She was doing this. She thought of that movie where the man pretended for his son that life under the Nazis was normal, beautiful even. Something about that seemed prescient now that she thought about it. You could fake your way to a lot.

Ruth told the children there were more pool floats in the garage. They returned with sagging plastic mini Oldenburgs. Archie put the little nub between his lips (it was meant to look like a doughnut, sprinkled, with a bite taken out of it), the effort of exhalation exposing the filigree of his ribs.

It was so unfair, how much more capable Archie was. Three years of advantage. Rose couldn't get a single breath into her float, which was just a round raft, but looked comfortable. It was annoying. Archie was basically a grown-up, and she was stuck being just herself.

"I'll do it, honey." Amanda took the limp thing between her legs and, perched on the edge of the wooden chaise, coaxed it into shape.

"I like the doughnut one better." Nothing went her way and she couldn't stop herself from noting it.

"Too slow, stupid." Archie tossed the ring onto the surface of the pool. He bounced from the diving board, landing only half on the thing as though he'd meant to. He was unbothered by his sister's protests, had long learned how to ignore most of the things his sister had to say.

"The raft is more comfortable." Rose was the sort of plain, chubby girl Ruth couldn't help feel sorry for. Ruth thought Archie so like every boy she'd seen troop through the halls of her school, convinced of his own charms. Maybe this was something mothers did to sons. She worried about her grandsons, mothered/ smothered twice over.

Rose was old enough to know how to feign manners. Still, she whined. "But the doughnut is funny." Rose spoke in that particular mode kids deploy when appealing to adults who are not their parents.

"Funny is no good in the long run." At the umbrellaed table, Ruth crossed her legs. She wore her clean things. She'd stalked into the master bedroom, wincing at the unmade bed, the spent washcloths on the bathroom floor, the scattered dirty laundry. She felt better. Almost relaxed.

"This is harder than it looks." Amanda thought of Clay's cigarettes, stealing her breath. She knew it wasn't fair, not to have a vice. The modern world was so joyless. When had they turned into parents to each other?

Rose was impatient as any thirteen-year-old. "Mom, hurry."

She pulled the translucent nipple, shining with saliva, from her mouth. "Here you go." That was good enough.

Rose stood on the steps, tepid water to her shins. She and Archie vanished into their game, the private conspiracy of childhood. Children sided with one another, the future against the past.

Amanda often thought that siblings were like long-married couples, all those shorthand arguments. This endured only in childhood. She had little to do with her brothers beyond the occasional too-long email from her older brother, Brian, the rare misspelled text messages from her younger brother, Jason. "How long has he been gone?" Amanda checked her phone. At least the clock was working.

"Twenty minutes?" G. H. looked at his own watch. It was that long into town, more if you drove slowly, as a man who didn't know the place might. "He'll be back soon."

"Should I make lunch?" Amanda was less hungry than bored.

"I can help." Ruth was already on her feet. Hard to discern even to her whether she wanted to or felt she had to. She did like cooking, but was that because convention forced her into the kitchen until she'd learned to enjoy time spent there?

"The more the merrier." Amanda didn't want the woman's company, but maybe it would distract her from thinking about her husband.

It was cooler inside, though Ruth had adjusted the thermostat so that it wasn't too cold. She felt this was wasteful. "You shouldn't worry, you know."

This was a kindness, Amanda understood. Clay had bought brie and chocolate. There were sandwiches, a particular favorite of Rose's, a recipe he used to make on New Year's Day for some reason; traditions just begin, somehow, then they end. "I'll warn you, this recipe sounds odd, but it's so good." She laid out ingredients.

Ruth was the one who submerged the Thanksgiving bird in salty water. She was the one who stretched bacon on the rack and let it crisp in the oven. She was the one who used a knife to sunder the flesh from the grapefruit's membranes. This was her room. "Chocolate?"

Amanda looked at the things arrayed on the counter, each individual chocolate chip somehow lovely, the soft wedge of cheese remarkable. "Salty and sweet, some kind of magic there."

"Opposites attract, I guess." Was Ruth flirting? Maybe she was. Were she and Amanda actually opposites? Random circumstance had brought them together, but wasn't everything random circumstance in the end? She chopped basil.

Ruth filled a bucket with ice. She produced cloth napkins, folded them into precise squares, and laid these out on a tray.

Amanda sniffed the fragrant tips of her fingers. "You're the gardener?"

"You won't catch George doing any of that old-people stuff." Ruth thought her more grandmotherly inclinations—the crossword, gardening, fat paperback histories of the Tudors—didn't seem evidence of anything. She was just a woman who liked what she liked. She wasn't old.

Amanda tried to guess. "He's in law? No, finance. No, law." She thought the expensive watch and neatly groomed salt-and-pepper hair and fine spectacles and luxurious shoes explained just what type of man G. H. was.

"Private equity. Should I slice this cheese?" Ruth had explained this before many times. It still meant very little to her. So what? G. H. didn't understand the particulars of what she had done at Dalton. Maybe no one, however much in love, cares about the minutiae of someone else's life. "So, finance, you could say. But not for a big bank. A small firm, a boutique operation."

This was her way of explaining it to people who were as confused as she was.

"Just slice it thin, for a grilled sandwich." They had enough for four but not precisely enough for six. She'd make one and leave it aside for Clay. For no reason but thinking of him, tears welled in her eyes. She wanted the news he would bring, but also she just wanted him back.

"At least the children are enjoying themselves." Ruth didn't want these people here, but she couldn't help but feel some human connection to them. Ruth worried about the world, but to care for other people felt something close to resistance. Maybe this was all they had.

Amanda melted butter in the black skillet. "There's that." Archie was almost a man. A century ago, he'd have been sent to the trenches of Europe. Should she tell him what was happening, and what would she tell him if she did?

"I found this onion dip. Maybe as a snack?" Ruth took out a bowl and a big spoon, and they worked in silence.

Amanda could not bear it, and so she broke it. "What do you think is happening out there?"

"Your husband will be back soon. He'll find out something." Ruth tasted the dip with her pinkie, an elegant gesture. She didn't want to play guessing games. She suspected Amanda didn't believe them. Ruth didn't want to be embarrassed.

Amanda removed a finished sandwich. "My kids rely on their phones to tell them how the weather is. To tell them what time it is, everything about the world around them, they can't even see the world anymore but through that prism." But even Amanda did this. She'd mocked the television commercial in which Zooey Deschanel seemed not to know whether it was raining, but she'd done the very same thing. "Without our phones, it turns out we're basically marooned out here." That's what it was. The feeling was withdrawal. On planes, she turned off airplane mode and started trying to check her email once you heard that ding that meant you were fewer than ten thousand feet aloft. The flight attendants were buckled in and couldn't scold. She'd pull and pull and pull at the screen, waiting for the connection to be established, waiting to see what she had missed.

"You'll believe it when you can see it on your phone." Ruth didn't even blame her for this. All these years debating the objectivity of fact had done something to everyone's brains.

"We just don't know anything. I'll feel better once we do. Do you think it's taking Clay a long time?"

Ruth put the dirty spoon in the sink. "There's an old idea, you're trapped on a desert island. You're far from society and people and maybe you have to choose the ten books or records you can take with you. Sort of makes the thing seem like paradise instead of a trap." A desert island sounded nice to her, though the seas were rising; maybe all such islands would vanish.

"But I don't have ten books. If we had the internet, I could get into my account and download all the books I've bought for my Kindle. But we don't have that." What she didn't say: We have the pool, these brie and chocolate sandwiches, and though we're strangers to one another, sure, we have one another too.

18

Amanda brought out wine. It was a vacation. Also: the hair of the dog. When the children complained it was too early to eat, Amanda let them vanish into their game, relieved. She poured pale pink wine into acrylic glasses and handed them around, ceremonial, almost religious. Someone attentive and patient had pressed the cloth napkins. She wondered if it had been Ruth.

"Your children are so polite." G. H. considered this the highest of praise.

"Thank you." Amanda was not sure this was not flattery, or just something to say, but she was pleased. "You've got a daughter?"

"Maya. She teaches Montessori in Massachusetts."

G. H. still wasn't entirely certain what this entailed, but he adored her.

"She runs the school. She doesn't just teach. She's in charge of the whole operation." Ruth bit into a baby carrot. She felt light. Maybe some part of her remembered reading once that people with fatal diagnoses entered a period of remission, calm, almost good health, once that's been established. A honeymoon. An interlude of joy.

"That's wonderful. We used to send Archie to a Montessori when he was small. It was amazing. Changing into their inside shoes. Washing hands. Saying good morning like colleagues at the office." She'd loved how he'd referred to play as "work." Those bumbling toddlers practicing for adulthood by lifting glass beads with a teaspoon, sponging up lunchtime spills.

"They say it's important for development. Maya is very passionate about it. The boys will start there, goodness, in only a couple of weeks, I suppose it'll be." Ruth was defensive.

"It can't be already!" G. H. knew that every cliché turned out to be true, that they do, in fact, grow up so fast.

"September." Ruth said it with hope. Her mother would have brought God into it—*God willing*, a reflex like drawing breath. They hadn't scorned it, but they hadn't learned that woman's devotion. Maybe she was onto something. Maybe it was a folly to assume anything happened without someone—God, sure, why not him—willing it.

Why did Amanda think of the Earth, Wind and Fire song, or why did the thought seem racist? No, some of their best friends were not black. Their friend Peter was married to a woman named Martika, whose mother had been a famous black model in the 1970s. Their neighbor on the ground floor was black, but also transgender, or nonbinary, or—Amanda always referred to this person by name just to be safe: *Jordan, so good to see you; Jordan, how is your summer going?; Jordan, it's been so hot out lately.* "It does fly by. Older parents always said that to me when Archie was a baby, and I would think, Well, I can't wait for this to go by. Because I was exhausted. But now I realize they were right." She was babbling.

"I was about to say as much to you. You beat me to it. I remember Maya at this age." G. H. was wistful, but also he was worried. They'd had fine lives, long lives, happy lives. Maya and her family were the only thing that it amounted to, of course, and that was something. A father should protect, and as he'd driven the night before, he'd worked through what he might do for her from the distance of Long Island and realized there wasn't much. But Maya wasn't the one who needed help; they were. Maya and the boys were fine.

Ruth wondered what version of the girl was in her husband's mind. She didn't want to ask. It was too private in front of this stranger. It was odd enough that they were all sitting there in their swimsuits.

"It must be fun to be grandparents. You get to do all the spoiling and don't have to get up all night or scold them for bad report cards or whatever." Amanda's own parents discharged that office with indifference. They didn't dislike Archie and Rose, but they didn't dote upon them. They were two of seven cousins, and her parents had retired to Santa Fe, where her father painted terrible landscapes and her mother volunteered at a dog shelter. They were determined to enjoy the liberty of their old age in that strange place where it took longer for water to boil.

"These sandwiches are good." Ruth had doubted they would be. Also she wanted a change of subject. The truth was, Maya guarded Beckett and Otto. She thought her parents feeble, or conservative, unable to comprehend the philosophy of it, what she and Clara had agreed upon. Ruth would come bearing bags from Books of Wonder, and Maya would pore over them like a rabbi, searching out their sins. It was well intentioned. Her distrust was not of her parents but of the world that they had made, and maybe she was right. Ruth could not resist buying them adorable things— little gingham shirts, like you'd put onto a teddy bear—and Maya would try to conceal her disdain. No matter, Ruth just wanted to be humored, and hold the boys' clean-smelling bodies close against her own. It was remarkable, how that made her feel. Invincible.

"They are good," G. H. agreed.

"Well, we do some spoiling," she allowed. "When we get the chance." That's what she wanted, the chance to see her family.

Amanda no longer thought they were con men, but was this the precursor to dementia, the first warning sign, like keys left in the refrigerator or socks worn into the shower or thinking Reagan was still president? Wasn't that how it worked: first fiction, then paranoia, then Alzheimer's? She felt the same way about her parents—their volition seemed suspect. They'd moved to Santa Fe after skiing in New Mexico once or twice a decade earlier; it made no sense to her, and their contentment seemed a bit like delusion. "It's the whole point of being a grandparent."

"George is worse than I am—"

"Wait." She was more rude than she'd meant to be, and gave the people a sheepish look. "I just realized. Your name is *George Washington*?"

There was no particular shame in it. He'd been explaining it for sixty-plus years. "My name is George
Herman Washington."

"I'm sorry. That was rude of me." It was the wine,
maybe? "It's just that it seems somehow fitting." She
couldn't explain it, but maybe it was self-evident;
someday there would be an anecdote, the time she sat
poolside with a black man named George Washington
while her husband went forth to figure out what had
gone wrong in the world. They'd traded their disaster stories the night before, and this would just be one
more of those.

"No apologies necessary. Part of the reason I settled
on using my initials early in my career."

"It's a fine name." Ruth was not insulted, just marveled at the familiarity with which this woman talked
to them. She knew it made her sound even more like
an old woman, but she missed a sense of propriety
about things.

"It is that! A fine name. And wonderful initials, I
think. G. H. sounds like a captain of industry, a master
of his business. I would trust a G. H. with my money."
Amanda was overcompensating now, but also a little
tipsy, the wine, the heat, the strangeness. "Clay should
be back soon, don't you think?" She looked at her wrist
but was not wearing her watch.

19

The children were bored by their leisure. Outnumbered, Archie and Rose rediscovered some connection, were again a five-year-old and two-year-old cooperating toward some unstated goal. They'd left the pool, left the grown-ups, were into the grass, the shade the relief the pool had not been.

"Let's go in the woods, Archie." She thought about what she'd seen. It didn't make sense, even to her. "I saw something this morning. Deer."

"They're everywhere, dumbass. They're like squirrels or pigeons. Who cares." She wasn't terrible, his sister, and she was still a little kid, so she couldn't help being a dumbass. Had he been that stupid at thirteen?

"No. I mean like. Come on." Rose looked over her shoulder at the adults eating lunch. She couldn't say

"Please" because begging would turn him off. She had to make it sound appealing. She wanted to pretend they were exploring, but they actually would be exploring, so it wasn't even a game. "Let's see what's out there."

"There's nothing out there." Still, he kind of wondered what was out there. Indian arrowheads? Money? Strangers? He'd found, in various woods he'd visited in his life, some weird shit. Three pages torn from a dirty magazine: a lady with old-fashioned hair, tan skin, immense boobs, pouting and bending her body this way and that. A dollar bill. A jar filled with not-quite-clear liquid he was sure was piss but didn't know how to prove that because he didn't want to open a jar that might contain someone else's piss. There were mysteries in the world, was all Rosie was saying, and he knew it but didn't want to hear it from her.

"What if there is? Maybe there's a house back there." She was imagining something as yet unclear even to her.

"There's no other houses anywhere near here." Archie said it like he couldn't believe it, or like he regretted it. He understood. He was bored too.

"There's that farm. We saw them selling the eggs, remember?" Maybe those farmers had kids, maybe they had a daughter, maybe her name was Kayla or Chelsea or Madison and maybe she had her own phone, and maybe she had money, or an idea for something that would be fun to do. Maybe she'd invite them inside, and it would be air-conditioned, and they would play video games, and eat Fritos, and drink Diet Coke with ice cubes in it.

Rose was hot and itchy. She wanted to go into the woods with her brother, to go where the adults couldn't see them, bother them. She imagined evidence out there. Footprints. Tracks. Proof.

Archie retrieved a stick from the ground, heaved it into the trees like a javelin. Kids loved sticks the way dogs did. Take a kid to the park, and they pick up a stick. Some kind of animal response.

"There's a swing. Cool." It hung from a tall tree. There was a small shed that could have been a playhouse or full of tools. Beyond, the grass ebbed until there was nothing but dirt and trees. Rose trotted toward it and sat.

Archie swore and felt like a man, complaining about the knots and rocks under his feet. "Shit."

"What's in that thing?" Something about the shed made Rose cautious. Anything could be inside it. Rose had started pretending, or she never stopped pretending.

"Let's open it and see." Archie sounded confident but privately shared his sister's awe at the thing. It could have been the playhouse of some kid who was dead now. There could be a person inside it, waiting for them to open the door. It was something from a movie, or the kind of story they didn't want their life stories to be.

The adults were behind the fence; it was like they had ceased to be. Rose hopped from the swing and stepped toward the little structure. She broke a spiderweb, invisible until it was not, felt that terrible shiver you do in that moment. The body knew what it was doing. It was scaring you away in case the spider was poisonous. She told herself not to scream—her brother had no patience for girlie things like that. A sound emerged all the same, a kind of strangled disgust.

"What?" Archie looked at his sister, some concern mixed with his disdain. That, too, was an animal response, the big brother's.

"Spiderweb." She thought of *Charlotte's Web*. She knew spiders did not have human personalities and voices, but worried about the spider she might have displaced, could not but imagine it a kindly female spider. She did not know that she limned generosity with femininity, part of the moral of that particular story. She did not know that her mother objected to that, when rereading it aloud a few years ago, when they were small enough to be read to at night.

The boy and the girl moved together through the thick grass, their bodies near naked and pinked from the sun, prickled from the cooler air beneath the boughs, goose fleshed from the spider's silk and the fear that was the best part of exploration. Seen from far away, they looked as the fawns did when you saw them early in the morning, young, hesitant, ungainly, but graceful for being only what they were.

Archie thought, but did not say, *Pussy.* It was a reflexive response to the perception of weakness, but she was his little sister. "Open it."

Rose hesitated and then did not. She had to be brave, that was the game. There was the kind of notch you depress with your thumb, over a handle she gripped but lightly. The metal was weathered, and the touch felt charged. Rose pulled open the door, which made a loud creak. Inside: nothing, a scattering of dried leaves in the corner that looked almost deliberate. Rose's heart was thudding so that she could hear it. "Oh." She was a little disappointed, though she couldn't say what she had expected to find in there.

Archie ducked his head into the building, but did not enter it. "This stupid fucking place is so boring."

"Yeah." Rose dug into the ground with a toenail that had been painted pale blue weeks before.

Now Archie understood it was an improvisatory game. "Maybe this is just where he sleeps, though. Where he hides at night."

Immediately afraid. "Who?"

He shrugged his shoulders. "Whoever made that impression." Archie pointed at the leaves, which had once been wet but had dried into a thick, contoured surface. "I mean, if you were in these woods with nowhere to go and no place to sleep—what would you do?"

She didn't want to think about it. "What do you mean?"

"You couldn't like—climb a tree, and sleep up there. But anywhere on the ground would be like—unsafe. Snakes and shit like that. Rabid animals. Four walls! And a roof. It's basically luxurious. And there's this window—" Archie gestured at the dirty pane cut into the side of the shed, which they had not noticed until they opened it.

"Yeah, I guess." She definitely wouldn't want to sleep outside. She couldn't imagine sleeping in the branches of a tree. She didn't think she could even climb a tree. They'd done rock climbing at Park Slope Day Camp a couple of years ago. She'd been tethered at her waist, had worn a helmet and kneepads, but still refused to go on halfway up the wall, hanging there shrieking until her counselor Darnell worked the rope to get her back down.

Archie paused meaningfully. ". . . So he can see."

"See what?"

Archie bent back into the shed, looked through the window. "Into the house, of course. See for yourself. There's a perfect view."

Rose stepped forward, recoiling a little at the bare dirt under her feet. She did not have to bend, she was not as tall as her brother, but she did, her hand on his forearm to steady her. She could, in fact, see the house from that vantage.

He went on. "Isn't that . . . the room you're sleeping in? Wow. Correct me if I'm wrong. But I'm pretty sure it is. Just imagine, when it's dark out here but the house is all lit up. Your little bedside lamp is glowing, and you're reading, nice and cozy under the covers. He could just follow that light right up to you. I bet you could see right in the windows without even having to stand on tiptoe."

She pulled her body back, knocking her head against the threshold. "Shut up, Archie."

He stifled a laugh.

"Just shut up." She folded her arms against her chest. "Listen. This morning I saw deer. Not a deer. A lot of deer. A hundred. Maybe more. Right here. It was so weird. Do they go around in big groups like that?"

Archie walked toward the tree in whose shade the little playhouse was nestled. He reached up and leaped just slightly, took hold of the lowest limb, lifted his knees to his chest, and swung, animal and mischievous. He dropped to the ground with a thud. He spat into the dust. "I don't fucking know anything about fucking deer."

Peach-colored, fuzzed, sticky, their bodies dissolved into the foliage; they couldn't be seen, heard, spied, as they investigated.

They wanted something to happen, but something was happening. They did not know it, and it did not involve them, not really. It would, of course; the world belonged to the young. They were babes in the woods, and if the tale were to be believed, they would die, the birds would see to their bodies, maybe escort their souls to heaven. It depended on which version of the story you knew. The dark that had settled on Manhattan, that tangible thing, could be explained. But beyond the dark was everything else, and that was more vague, hard to hold on to as spider's silk, there but not there, all around them. They walked farther into the woods.

20

It had been fourteen minutes since he'd left the house. He remembered checking the display as he started the car. Maybe it was sixteen. Maybe he was misremembering. Maybe it was fewer! Then he'd stopped to smoke that cigarette, which he usually said took seven minutes but actually took closer to four. So Clay had been driving for ten minutes, which was not really so long, and meant he couldn't truly be lost. He told himself to calm down, then pulled the car into the McKinnon Farms driveway to smoke a cigarette. He could, of course, continue down the drive, to the farmhouse or some other building where people would be, but that would mean he was truly panicked, which he was not. So he smoked and tried to find the relaxation inherent in the act, then stubbed the thing out before it was truly done, impatient. He couldn't re-member, when they'd driven to the house that first day, if theirs had been the only car. That first day seemed weeks in the past.

He closed the door harder than he meant to, though it was not exactly a slam. It was loud enough to under-score the general quiet. He told himself that this was normal, and it was. It would have seemed peaceful had he been prepared to find peace. It seemed irritating at best and menacing at worst. Symbols don't mean any-thing; you invest them with meaning, depending on what you most need. Clay chewed a piece of gum and started the car. He turned left out of the farm's access road and drove slowly, noting every possible turn on the right. There was one, then another, then, finally, another, but none looked familiar, and none were adja-cent to a stand selling eggs. There was a sign that read only "Corn," but this didn't seem to indicate anything at all, and must have been old.

He thought of the mental and actual preparation they'd put in to prepare Archie to ride the subway alone. The way they'd insisted the boy memorize their phone numbers, in case his telephone was lost or bro-ken, the plan they'd agreed upon should he find him-self on a rerouted train bound for some part of the city where he'd never been. Now he rode the subway all the time. Clay rarely thought about it. That was how it worked, maybe. You prepared your child to sleep through the night or wield a fork or piss in the toilet or say please or eat broccoli or be respectful to adults, and then the child was prepared. That was the end of it. He didn't know why he was thinking about Archie, and he shook his head as though to clear it. He would have to turn around and take one of the three, four, five turn-offs he'd passed, determine where they led, see if they were the right way. One of them had to be. He needed only to be methodical. He'd trace the route back to the house, then begin again, more cautious, more attentive, and work his way to town, where he had intended all along to end up. He really wanted that Coke now. His head hurt from lack of caffeine.

Their vacation was ruined. The spell had been broken. Truly, what he should do was drive back to the house and have the kids pack their things. They'd be back in the city before dinner. They could splurge at that French place on Atlantic, order the fried anchovy, the steak, a martini. Clay was only decisive after the fact. And now he was—well, he would say turned around, not lost. He felt a strangely powerful desire to see his children.

He took the first left, and drove only a few yards before understanding that this was not the route; it pitched uphill, and he knew the road had been level. He turned the car around and turned back onto the main road, barely slowing, knowing there was no traffic coming in either direction. He took the second left, and this seemed like it might be the way. He drove on, then turned right, because he could. Perhaps that was it, and the painted egg shack was just up that road. Everything looked familiar because trees and grass only ever looked precisely as you'd expect them to.

He turned the car around again, went back to the road onto which he'd turned from the main road, and there, across that main road, he saw a woman. She was wearing a white polo shirt and khaki pants. On some women it would have looked like leisure wear, but on this woman, her face a broad, indigenous shape (ancient blood, timeless dignity), it looked like a uniform. The woman saw him, raised a hand, waved at him, gestured at him, beckoned him. Clay pulled into the road, more slowly now, and glided to a stop. He lowered the passenger window and smiled out at the woman, the way you're taught to smile at dogs so you don't betray your fear of them.

"Hello, there!" He wasn't sure what he'd say. Would he admit to being lost?

"Hello." She looked at him and then began speaking, very quickly, in Spanish.

"I'm sorry." He shrugged. It sounded, he hated to admit even in his private thoughts, like gibberish. He didn't speak any other languages. Clay didn't even like to attempt it. It made him feel like a fool, or a child.

The woman continued. The words poured out of her. She barely took a breath. She had something urgent to say, and had maybe forgotten what English she possessed—*hello* and *thank you* and *it's ok* and *Windex* and *telephone* and *text* and *Venmo* and the days of the week. She talked. She kept talking.

"I'm sorry." He shrugged again. He did not understand, of course. But maybe he comprehended. Oh, that was a word: *comprende.* They said it in movies. You couldn't live in this country and not know some Spanish. If he'd had time to think about it, if he'd forced himself to calm down, he could have communicated with this woman. But she was panicked, and she was panicking him. He was lost and wanted his family. He wanted a steak at that restaurant on Atlantic Avenue. "No Spanish."

She said more. Something something. He heard *beer* but she said *deer*; they sound alike in both tongues. She said more. She said *telephone*, but he didn't understand. She said *electric*, but he didn't hear. Tears welled at the corners of her small eyes. She was short, freckled, broad. She could have been fourteen or forty.

Her nose was running. She was weeping. She spoke louder, hurried, was imprecise, maybe lapsing out of Spanish altogether into some dialect, something still more ancient, the argot of civilizations long dead, piles of rubble in jungles. Her people discovered corn, tobacco, chocolate. Her people invented astronomy, language, trade. Then they'd ceased to be. Now their descendants shucked the corn they'd been the first to know about, and vacuumed rugs and watered decorative beds of lavender planted poolside at mansions in the Hamptons that sat unused most of the year. She forgot herself, even, put her hands on his car, which they both knew was a violation. She held on to the two-inch lip of window that was sticking up out of the door. Her hands were small and brown. She was still talking through the tears; she was asking him a question, a question he could not understand and anyway would not have been able to answer.

"I'm sorry." He shook his head. If his phone had worked, he might have tried Google Translate. He could have urged her to get into the car, but how would he have made her understand that he was lost, not driving in circles because he meant to kill her or lull her to sleep, as suburban parents did with their infants? A different man would respond differently, but Clay was the man he was, one unable to provide what this woman needed, one afraid of her urgency, her fear, which did not need translation. She was afraid. He should be afraid. He was afraid. "I'm sorry." He said it to himself, more than to her. She released the window as he started to roll it up. He drove farther down the road, quickly, though he'd intended to investigate all those driveways. He needed to be away from her more even than he needed to be with his family.

21

In the woods you had this sense of something you couldn't see no matter how you tried. There were bugs, dun-colored toads holding still, mushrooms in fantastical shapes that seemed accidental, the sweet smell of rot, inexplicable damp. You felt small, like one of many things, and the least important too.

Maybe, maybe, something had happened to them. Maybe something was happening to them. For centuries there was no language to describe the fact that tumors blossomed inside lungs, beautiful volunteers like flowering plants that take root in unlikely places. Not knowing what to call it did not change it, death by drowning as your chest filled with sacs of liquid.

Rose felt eyes on her, but then she pretended, often, that she was being watched. She saw herself at the remove of a cell-phone camera. She was young and didn't understand that was how everyone saw themselves, as the main character of a story, rather than one of literal billions, our lungs slowly filling with salt water.

In the woods, the light was different. The trees interfered with it. The trees were alive and felt like Tolkien's majestic creatures. The trees were watching, and not impartially. The trees knew what was up. The trees talked amongst themselves. They were sensitive to the seismic reverberations of bombs far distant. Trees miles away—where the ocean had begun to breach the land—were dying, though it would take years for them to be reduced to albino logs. The trees had all the time the rest of us do not. The mangroves could outsmart it, pull up their roots like a Victorian lady's skirts, sip the salt from the ground, so maybe they'd be fine, with the alligators and the rats and the roaches and the snakes. Maybe they'd be better off without us. Sometimes, sometimes, suicide is a relief. That was the right noun for what was happening. The sickness in the ground and in the air and in the water was all a clever design. There was a menace in the woods and Rose could feel it, and another child would have called it God. Did it matter if a storm had metastasized into something for which no noun yet existed? Did it matter if the electrical grid broke apart like something built of Lego?

Did it matter if Lego would never biodegrade, would outlast Notre Dame, the pyramids at Giza, the pigment daubed on the walls at Lascaux? Did it matter if some nation claimed responsibility for the outage, did it matter that it was condemned as an act of war, did it matter if this was pretext for a retaliation long hoped for, did it matter that proving who had done what via wires and networks was actually impossible? Did it matter if an asthmatic woman named Deborah died after six hours trapped on an F train stalled beneath the Hudson River, and that the other people on the subway walked past her body and felt nothing in particular? Did it matter that machines meant for supporting life ceased doing that hard work after the failure of backup generators in Miami, in Atlanta, in Charlotte, in Annapolis? Did it matter if the morbidly obese grandson of the Eternal President actually did send a bomb, or did it matter simply that he could, if he wanted to?

The children couldn't know that some of this had happened. That in an old-age home in a coastal town called Port Victory a Vietnam vet named Peter Miller was floating facedown in two feet of water. That Delta had lost a plane traveling between Dallas and Minneapolis during the disruption of the air traffic control system. That a pipeline was spilling crude onto the ground in an unpopulated part of Wyoming. That a major television star had been struck by a car at the intersection of Seventy-Ninth and Amsterdam and died because the ambulances couldn't get anywhere. They couldn't know that the silence that seemed so relaxing in the country seemed so menacing in the city, which was hot, still, and quiet in a way that made no sense. Nothing matters to children but themselves, or perhaps that is the human condition.

Barefoot, bareheaded, bare-breasted, the children moved gingerly, feet arching, toes recoiling. Branches grazed their skin, and you could not see the marks they made. The illness of the planet had never been a secret, the nature of it all had never been in doubt, and if something had changed (it had), the fact that they didn't yet know it had no bearing on the matter at all. It was inside them now, whatever it was. The world operated according to logic, but the logic had been evolving for some time, and now they had to reckon with that. Whatever they thought they'd understood was not wrong but irrelevant.

"Archie, look." It came out as a whisper. She'd lowered her voice, assuming respect, as you might inside a holy place. She pointed. A roof. A clearing that became a lawn. A brick house, like the one where they were staying, a pool, a sturdy wood swing set.

"A house." He wasn't even derisive, just declarative.

Archie hadn't been expecting to find anything. Ruth had told them there was nothing out here, but they had gone farther than Ruth ever had, were curious about the world in a way Ruth was not. This was a satisfying discovery. Other people. Archie had left his phone charging in his bedroom. He wished he'd brought it, tried to borrow these people's WiFi.

"Should we go up there?" She was thinking of the swing set and that maybe the kids had outgrown it. She was thinking that not talking to strangers was a matter for the city only.

"Nah. Let's go." Archie turned toward what he believed was the direction from which they'd come. He didn't feel the tick burrowing into his ankle any more than he could Earth's deliberate daily rotation. He didn't feel anything in the air because it felt unchanged.

They walked, not slowly, but not in a hurry. Time passed differently in the woods. They didn't know how long they'd been gone. They didn't know what they'd intended to do. They didn't know why it felt satisfying, just strolling through the shade of the trees, air and sun and bugs and sweat on skin. They didn't know that their father was even then driving past, less than a half a mile away, less than a quarter mile, near enough they could run to him, save him. From where they stood they couldn't hear the road, and they weren't thinking about their father, their mother, anyone.

As they walked, Archie and Rose barely spoke, mucking through the leaves, shivering a little. Their bodies knew what their minds did not. Children and the very old have this in common. Born, you understand something about the world. That's why toddlers report conversing with ghosts and unnerve their parents. The very old begin to remember it, but can rarely articulate it, and no one listens to the very old anyway.

They were not afraid, the children, not really. They were at peace. A change was upon them; a change was upon it all. What you called it didn't matter. Overhead, the leaves shifted and sighed, and there was the sound of Archie and Rose saying something to each other, something impossible to make out, something that existed only between them, the private language of youth. And save that there was only the gentle rustle of the trees adjusting their limbs and the susurrus of unseen insects. Those would settle, soon, the way that things grow quiet before the sudden summer rainstorm, because the bugs knew, and would hold their bodies tight to the stippled bark of the trees and wait for whatever was coming.

22

So he'd been gone for forty-five minutes. It meant he'd stopped to smoke. It meant he'd stopped for groceries. Amanda: What, me worry?

Ruth put a bowl of cherries, more black than red, onto the table. It had the air of ceremony.

"Thank you." Amanda didn't know why she was thanking the woman. Hadn't she spent eleven dollars on these cherries?

A cloud, one of those soft, cottony ones, all curves like a child's drawing, seeped across the sky. The change was severe enough that G. H. shivered. "I could almost use a minute in the hot tub."

Amanda took this for an invitation. She left the table, sank into the froth beside the strange man. The water made you buoyant, and so it made it hard to sit.

Amanda leaned forward to look toward the trees. She could not see the children any longer.

"They're fine, I expect." George understood. You had a child and were forever vigilant. "There's nothing back there but more trees."

Ruth looked at the two of them. Wine with lunch had made her drowsy. "I might make some coffee then."

"That would be nice, love, thank you."

Amanda smiled. "Can I do anything?"

"You relax." Ruth went back into the house.

"The pool. The hot tub. They cost a fortune in electric bills. We're going to have solar panels put up. I didn't want to do it during the season, when we use the house. I'm waiting until September, October. My contractor told me he generates enough that he sells power back to the grid. More people should do that." G. H. was almost beginning to enjoy this woman's company. He liked an audience.

"Clean energy. Should save the planet. Should be a law." Sometimes at the movie theater or on the sidewalk Amanda would see wind energy proselytizers with pamphlets and free buttons, but it always seemed like a scam. "How did you get into your line of work?" More small talk.

"I had a mentor, in college. It was him who made

me—I mean, I didn't know what people did for a living. My mother ran a hair salon." His tone conveyed his respect for his mother's work. She died of cancer—liver, stomach, pancreas—probably from handling the chemicals women like her used to make their hair respectable. "Stephen Johnson. Gone now, but what a life."

"I guess it's like having a green thumb. Or being good at doing the Rubik's cube. Some people can make money, some people can't." She knew who she and Clay were.

This was one of G. H.'s hobbyhorses. "That's the conventional wisdom. You have to ask yourself why that is. Who wants you to believe that it's not possible to get, if not rich, at least comfortable? It's a skill. You can be taught. It's just about information. You have to read the paper. You have to listen to what is happening in the world." Of course, he thought you had to be *smart*, but he considered that a given.

"I read the paper." She was a woman of the world, she believed. She wanted to say something about her work, but there was little to say.

"You only have to understand the patterns that govern the world. Did you ever hear about that guy who beat the game show *Press Your Luck*?" G. H. looked down at her over the rims of his Ray-Bans. He wanted a newspaper now. He thought of the numbers. He wondered what had moved.

"Whammy? No Whammy?"

"All he did was pay attention and learn that the Whammy wasn't random at all. It always appeared in a certain sequence. That information was just there, but no one had ever bothered to look for it." Rich people didn't have a moral authority. They just knew where the Whammy was.

"That's interesting," she said, indicating that she did not find it so at all. Where were the kids? "I'm glad to be away from my work, for the moment. Don't get me wrong—it's interesting, to me, anyway, helping people tell the stories of their companies, helping them find consumers, make that connection. But it's a lot of diplomacy. It gets tiring."

George went on. "My mentor was one of the first black men at a Wall Street firm. We had lunch one afternoon—lunch! I was twenty-one." How to communicate that he'd never previously considered eating lunch at a restaurant, never mind one like that, carpeted, mirrored, brass ashtrays and solicitous uniformed girls in ponytails? He'd showed up without a tie, and Stephen Johnson took him to Bloomingdale's, bought him four from Ralph Lauren. G. H. hadn't known how to put them on; the ones he'd worn at Christmas were clip-on.

"I've always thought that women need to stick together in the workforce. Or maybe everywhere. I'd be nowhere without my mentors." This was not entirely true. Amanda had worked for women, but secretly preferred working with men. Their motivations were so simple.

"He said to me, 'We're all machines.' That's it. You get to choose the nature of the machine you are. We're all machines, but some of us are smart enough that we get to determine our programming." What he'd said: Fools believe rebellion is possible. Capital determines everything. You can either calibrate yourself to that or think you've rejected it. But the latter, Stephen Johnson said, was a delusion. You were either going to get rich or not. You only had to choose. Stephen Johnson and he were the same kind of person. He was who he was— patriarch, intellect, husband, collector of fine watches, first-class traveler—because he'd chosen to be.

Amanda was lost. They were talking around each other, not to each other. "You must love what you do."

Did he care about it, or had he come to care about it, as the spouses in an arranged marriage find, over time, a transaction settled into something like affection? "I'm a lucky man."

The heat was clarifying in the way of orgasm, akin to blowing your nose. The hot sun, the hot water, but still this energy: she could have run around the block, or taken a nap, or done pull-ups. She was waiting for Clay to drive up the road. It had been an hour, right? She listened for the sound of the car.

They should leave. If they timed it right, they'd be home for dinner. They could treat themselves to one of the neighborhood restaurants that was just slightly too expensive to be a regular haunt. She didn't know, of course, that Clay had the same thought. She didn't know this bespoke how well suited to each other they were.

The yard was quiet but for the steamy undulation of the tub. She looked at the woods, and she thought she saw something moving but couldn't pick out their bodies. She thought a mother should be able to do that, once upon a time, but then she'd actually taken the toddlers to the playground and lost them immediately, a sea of small humanity that had nothing to do with her. She was happy the children had each other, were still children enough to get lost in their games, tromping through the woods like she imagined country kids did.

She was sitting there, not doing anything more, when it happened, when there was something. A noise, but that didn't cover it. Noise was an insufficient noun, or maybe noise was always impossible to describe in words. What was music but noise; could words get at Beethoven? This was a noise, yes, but one so loud that it was almost a physical presence, so sudden because of course there was no precedent. There was nothing (real life!), and then there was a noise. Of course they'd never heard a noise like that before. You didn't hear such a noise; you experienced it, endured it, survived it, witnessed it. You could fairly say that their lives could be divided into two: the period before they'd heard that noise and the period after. It was a noise, but it was a transformation. It was a noise, but it was a confirmation. Something had happened, something was happening, it was ongoing, the noise was confirmation even as the noise was mystery.

Understanding came after the fact. That was how life worked: I'm being hit by a car, I'm having a heart attack, that purple-gray thing emerging from between my legs is the head of our child. Epiphanies. They were the end of a chain of events invisible until that epiphany had been reached. You had to walk backward and try to make sense. That's what people did, that's how people learned. Yes. So. The thing was a noise.

Not a bang, not a clap. More than thunder, more than an explosion; none of them had never heard an explosion. Explosions seemed common because films so often depicted them, but explosions were rare, or they'd all been lucky to be spared proximity to explosions. All that could be said, in the moment, was that it was noise, big enough to alter forever their working definitions of noise. You'd cry if you weren't so scared, surprised, or affected in some way impossible to understand. You might cry even so.

The noise was quick, maybe, but the air buzzed with it for what seemed like a long time. What was the noise, and what was the noise's aftereffect? One of those unanswerable questions. Amanda stood up. Behind them, the glass pane of the door between the bedroom and the deck cracked, a fine but long crack, beautiful and mathematical and something no one would notice for a while yet. The noise was loud enough to make a man fall to his knees. That's what Archie did, distant, in the woods: fell to his bare knees. A noise that could make a person fall to their knees was only nominally a noise. It was something else for which there was no noun necessary, because how often would one use such a word?

"What the fuck?" This was, maybe, the only proper response. Amanda was not talking to George. She was not talking to anyone. "What the fuck?" She said it a third time, a fourth time, a fifth time, it didn't matter. She kept saying it, and it was unanswered, as a prayer.

Amanda was trembling. Not shaken but shaking, vibrating. She went quiet. A noise so big, how could you meet it but with silence? She thought what she was doing was screaming. The feeling of a scream, the emotion of a scream, but in fact she gasped, like a fish flipped out of its pond, the noise deaf-mutes make in moments of passion, the shadow, the silhouette, of speech. Amanda was angry.

"What—" She didn't feel any particular need to finish her sentence because she was talking to herself. "What. What. What."

George had leaped from the tub, didn't even cover his body with a towel. Everything in the world was quiet, except, maybe, that sense of afterglow, the void where the noise had only just been. Perhaps her ears were damaged, and it was an illusion. Perhaps her brain was damaged. There had been that story, about consular employees in Havana who developed neurological symptoms believed to be linked to noise. It had never occurred to Amanda that a weapon could be sonic, had never occurred to her that a noise might be something to fear. You told kids and pets not to worry during thunderstorms.

Amanda was shaking. There was a sharp taste, like

she had a Kennedy half dollar sitting on top of her tongue. If she moved, the noise might recur. If it did, she was not sure she would be able to bear it. She never wanted to hear it again. "What was that?" This was more to herself than anything. Was it localized—inside the house, within the perimeter—or was it something related to the weather or interstellar or the parting of the heavens to herald the arrival of God himself? As she asked, she knew that the noise would never be satisfactorily explained. It was past logic, or explanation, at least.

It was very slow at first. She walked and then leaped down the steps. She had just been looking out at the trees. She tried to find their bodies in all that green and brown. She should call for them, and it seemed like she did, but she did not. Her voice did not work, or couldn't catch up to her body. She just moved. Slow, then fast, jog then run, Amanda went down past the pool, shoving open the gate, and into the grass. Her children, their perfect faces, their flawless bodies, were there, somewhere. She could see only the single mass of the landscape. It looked to her as it might had she been nearsighted and without her glasses, indistinct, bright, impossible.

She ran farther. The yard was not so big, there was not so much to run into. Still she did not call, only ran.

There was a little shed in the shadows. She pulled open the door and it was empty. All in one movement—she didn't truly stop running—she continued to the edge of the yard, soft dirt and dry leaves. The noise was over, but there was still a noise, her blood in her veins, her heart resilient enough. She needed her children's bodies against her own.

Amanda leaped over a stick, small enough that she could have stepped over it, and her feet were in the carpet of humus, here catching a pebble, pointed bark, a thorn, something wet and unpleasant. She should call out to them but didn't want to drown out their voices should they be calling to her, urgent *Mom*s, as convicts were said to utter upon their executions.

The kids, where were her kids? The trees barely seemed to move. They just stood, indifferent to her. Amanda sank to the ground. The touch of leaves, bark, dirt, was almost a comfort. The mud on her pink knees was almost a balm. The clean soles of her feet were blackened and pocked but not painful. At last she found herself. She intended to call out for the children, to call out the names they'd chosen so lovingly, but instead of "Archie" and "Rosie" (for the diminutive would surely have emerged, love and longing), Amanda only screamed, a terrible, animal scream, the second most shocking noise she had ever heard.

23

They spoke more quietly than normal. They were deferential, of course, to the noise. They were waiting for it to come back. They didn't want to be caught unawares, but how could you anticipate that, even having heard it before? All the same: there was disagreement.

G. H. did not wholly believe what he was saying. "It could have been thunder, I suppose." Sometimes you could will yourself to believe what you said.

"There are no clouds!" Amanda's fury was blunted, a bit, by relief. She had found her children, wide-eyed and filthy as mendicants, and would not let them go. She had Rose's right hand in hers as she used to, years ago, when the girl was misbehaving. On the girl's left hand the palm was etched red, a perfect, unbroken line.

Abraded skin on her left knee, smudges on her chin and shoulder and the soft midriff—she'd campaigned for months for a two-piece swimsuit—and greasy hair and red eyes, but otherwise the girl was fine. The children looked fine. They seemed fine.

Amanda had plunged headlong into the woods and found them by some instinct she'd forgotten she possessed, or perhaps it was dumb luck. The noise sent the three of them running, and their paths happened to intersect. The noise saw Clay stop the car beside the maddeningly empty road, open the door, and consider the heavens. The noise startled Ruth, filling the coffeepot, dropping a spoon to the ground. The noise bade those deer, more than a thousand in number, already heedless of the property lines drawn by men, to stampede through gardens without even stopping for a nibble. Homeowners were too distracted—by the shattered windows, by the screaming children, by the infant eardrums, irreparably affected—to gawk at all those animals.

Amanda and the children emerged from the woods, and though they were strangers there was real joy at their reunion. Ruth had put an arm around the boy's bare shoulders. G. H. had squeezed Amanda's forearm in paternal relief. The aftermath of the noise—a hum, a sense of vibration—seemed to linger. It was like a swarm of persistent insects, the biting flies you some-times encountered at the beach. There and not there. Dogged. Amanda suggested they go inside, articulating what everyone was feeling. The sky was quite blue and very pretty, but the out-of-doors seemed somehow untrustworthy. The noise seemed to belong to nature, but as Ruth knew, the bricks had not been enough to keep the sound away. "Was that a bomb?" Visions of mushroom clouds.

"Where's Dad?" Regressing as you did after a trauma, Archie's voice broke, high and awkward, on *Dad*. Where was Dad?

"He ran an errand." Amanda was terse.

"I'm sure he'll be back any moment." Ruth filled glasses with water. The children were filthy and sweaty. She wasn't sure how to help, and that was what she wanted to do. She couldn't hold her grandchildren close. She could get this stranger's children a glass of water.

"Thank you." Archie remembered his manners. That was a good sign.

"Why don't you go wash? I can stay with Archie." Ruth bent to pick up the dropped teaspoon with which she'd been measuring the coffee grounds. She wanted to help, but mostly she wanted a distraction.

Amanda took Rose to the bathroom, cleaned her

wounds. They were minor. The ritual was a comfort to both of them: damp toilet paper and Neosporin, her child's face close enough that she could smell her hot breath. After the genocide, beauty parlors helped Rwandans cope. Touching another human being was a curative. She swabbed the child's face with a damp washcloth, dressed her in a sweatshirt and shorts. Rose, who no longer wanted to be seen naked, did not even protest that. The noise had terrified her.

Ruth had to do *something*. "Drink your water, sweetie." The blandishment did not come naturally. At school, they called every child "friend." Even in trouble they were not subjected to "ma'am" and "sir" but "friend." Friend, we need to talk about your behavior. Friends, please lower your voices. It was holy in a non-committal way.

Archie's hairless back was coated with a paste of sweat and dust. You could have inscribed a word in the filth on his skin, the way pranksters wrote "Wash me" on untended cars. Dutiful, he took a sip. "My ears feel weird."

"It's probably normal." Ruth's ears didn't feel weird, but her everything else did. "That was—loud." It might have damaged their eardrums.

Amanda returned, the clean little girl holding her

hand, made a child again. "Oh Archie. You're a mess." She stroked his grimy back, reassured and reassuring.

G. H. peered out the window, suspicious of everything he could see, the pool, the rustling trees. That was all that was out there, that was all he could see, but he wasn't expecting to see—what? A bomb? A missile? Were those the same thing?

"Was it a plane?" Amanda was trying to reconstruct it, but a noise was like pain: your body couldn't remember its specifics. It might have been mechanical, and planes seemed the highest form of machine.

"A plane crashing?" Ruth didn't know if that was what she meant and couldn't guess what sort of sound it would make, a plane exploding like that one over Lockerbie or felled like the one that was destined for the US Capitol. Again she only had Hollywood films.

"Or breaking the sound barrier. A sonic boom. Was that a sonic boom?" They had flown on the Concorde once, a lark, their fifteenth anniversary. François Mitterand had been on their flight. "I think you can't break the sound barrier when you're over land. But it gets lost over the ocean. I think that's right."

"Planes don't usually break the sound barrier." Archie had done a report on it in sixth grade. "The Concorde doesn't fly anymore."

He was right in that the Concorde had only ever terrified the whales in the North Atlantic. But these were extraordinary times. He didn't know that the planes dispatched from Rome, New York, usually flew north, the most direct route to the open sea. But they were off to intercept something that approached the nation's eastern flank. The circumference of the noise they created was about fifty miles—a rend in heaven right over their little house.

Ruth had thought of it over their repast of strange sandwiches. "I noticed today—did you? There was no air traffic. Not one plane, not one helicopter."

G. H. knew, as his wife said it, that this was true. "You're right. I mean, usually we hear so many. Planes, helicopters."

"What do you mean?" Amanda asked. "There must have been—"

"Hobbyists taking lessons. Impatient people flying out from Manhattan. It's a big issue in the local op-eds." Ruth herself had become inured enough to the noise pollution that she noticed, instead, its absence. She didn't know what this meant, but thought it might mean something.

Amanda wanted to send the children out of the room, but there was no television to distract them. "Archie, why don't you go put on your clothes." Her hand on his gritty back. He was hot to the touch. "Drink more water. Maybe you should take a shower?"

Ruth understood; maybe any parent would. "Rose, maybe you should go lie down."

The girl didn't know if this strange woman was meant to be obeyed. She looked up at her mother to see what to do.

"That's a good idea, honey." Amanda was grateful. "Go curl up in Mommy's bed. Read your book."

"I'm going to go take a shower." Archie was suddenly conscious of being undressed. He couldn't confess this, but he'd pissed in his swimsuit when he heard that noise, like a baby. There was a point, when he was younger, where he'd dreamed of understanding grown-up conversation. Now he could, and realized he'd overestimated it. "Come on, Rose." A big brother's kindness.

Amanda waited until the children were gone. "What was that?"

Ruth looked past her husband to the window, the flat blue sky. "It's not the weather—" Ideal day for swimming, and anyway there had never been thunder so loud, that lasted so long. If they lived in Hawaii, she might have said it was a volcano.

G. H. was impatient. He was done with this. "We can agree that we don't know what it is," he said.

"Where is Clay?" Amanda looked at Ruth as though the woman were responsible. As the noise changed the girl from teen to child, it left Amanda soft, helpless.

Ruth had lost track of the time. "It wasn't so long ago. It just feels that way."

"He'll be back soon." G. H. was making promises.

"This settles it, though. Something is . . . happening." The lack of a cellular signal was an assault. The absence of television was a tactic. "We have to do something!"

"What should we do, sweetie?" Ruth didn't disagree, but she was at a loss.

"We're being attacked. This is an attack. What are you supposed to do in the event of an attack?"

"We're not being attacked." G. H. was not entirely certain, though, and it showed. "Nothing has changed."

"Nothing has changed?" Amanda was louder. "We're just sitting here, like, I don't know what. Is that what sitting ducks are? Ducks just sitting and waiting to be shot?" What a stupid expression. Why would a duck sit?

"I mean, we still don't know what's happening. We should just wait for Clay to come back, and we'll see what he's learned."

"Should I drive into town and look for Clay?" She didn't want to leave the house, but she would. Something had to be *done*. "Should we fill the bathtubs?

Do we have batteries and Tylenol? Should we find the neighbors? Is there enough food? Is this an emergency?"

G. H. put his brown hands on the Vermont stone countertops. "This is an emergency. We're prepared. And we are safe here." Those were the facts: his energy bars, his case of wine.

"Is there a generator? Is there a bomb shelter? Is there— I don't know. A hand-crank radio? One of those straws that makes it safe to drink dirty water?"

"He'll be back soon, I'm sure." G. H. was trying to convince himself as well. "We'll stay here. We're safe here. All of us. We'll stay here."

"It's fifteen minutes to town. Then fifteen minutes back. That's half an hour. At least." Ruth fidgeted. What were they doing? "Maybe it's longer if you don't know the way. Maybe it's twenty minutes. Forty, there and back."

Amanda was mad at all of them. "What if he's not coming back? What if the car died, or that noise did something to him, or—" What did she envision? Clay, gone forever.

"George is right. We're safe. Let's just sit tight."

"How can you say we're safe when you don't know what's happening to us?" Amanda hoped the children could not hear her. She wept, now.

"We heard that noise." Ruth was logical. "We should just wait. To see what we're going to have to do next."

Amanda was furious. "We don't have the internet, we don't have our phones, we don't know what anything is." She blamed it on these people. They'd knocked on the door and ruined everything.

"Maybe it was like—what was that? Ten Mile Island?" Ruth wanted a drink, but couldn't decide if this was a good idea. "There are power plants out here, aren't there?"

"Three Mile Island." G. H. always knew that sort of thing.

Amanda knew it from history books. "A nuclear accident?" The abiding fear of her youth: presidential red telephones, flashes of light, fallout. She'd forgotten all that at some point. "Oh my god. Should we tape the windows shut? Are we going to get sick?"

"I don't know that that would account for the noise." G. H. tried to remember: the steam was produced by the sea water used to cool the material that produced the reaction that created the energy. An earthquake in Japan had shown the fallacy; the sea water could flow back, poison could travel across the ocean. They'd found debris in Oregon. Would a nuclear incident make such a noise? Did the nuclear plants out here supply the city, and would their damage account for the blackout?

"A missile?" Amanda was thinking out loud. "North Korea. Ruth, you brought up North Korea."

"Iran." G. H. said it without meaning to.

"Iran?" Amanda said it like she'd never heard of the place.

"We shouldn't speculate." G. H. regretted it.

"Maybe this was. You know. The blackout then— the source of that noise, a bomb or whatever." Terrorists were planners. The action itself felt like impulse, because televisions couldn't show what preceded it: meetings, strategy, sketches, money. Those nineteen had practiced in flight simulators! Where would you even find a flight simulator?

"We're just getting worked up—" G. H. felt it was important to stick to what they could see.

Ruth would have a drink. She found the wine key. She went to the cabinet and took out a cabernet. "But . . . Clay. What if—what if he found something?" What was worse: he was not coming back, or he was, and had found something out in the world truly unbearable, worse than they were able to even guess at, and had to come back with news of it and force these people to bear it with him?

Amanda wept, more now. "But we won't know what is happening until we do. We're just . . ." She looked at the pendant lamps, new but made to look like something from a turn-of-the-century schoolhouse, at the clever cabinetry that concealed the stainless steel dishwasher, at the milk-glass bowl full of lemons. The house had seemed so alluring. It didn't feel as safe anymore, it didn't feel the same, nothing did.

"Maybe the television will come back on." Ruth tried to sound optimistic.

"Or our cell phones will work again." Amanda said it like a prayer. She looked down at the countertop, noticing, maybe for the first time, the beautiful abstraction of stone. It didn't seem strong or solid, but it did seem newly beautiful. That was something.

24

Masculine responsibility, Clay realized, was utter bullshit. The vanity in wanting to save them! That noise made him want to be at home. He didn't want to protect; he wanted to be protected. The noise brought tears, frustrated, irritated tears. He was turned around and felt utterly lost. He didn't even want to smoke, but he was slowing the car to a stop when it happened, when the skies opened up and this intangible thing fell all around them. He didn't notice if it startled the birds and squirrels and chipmunks and moths and frogs and flies and ticks. He was paying attention only to himself.

Clay idled there, because there was no traffic to block. He waited eight minutes, sure the noise would come back. It did, but over Queens; distant enough that he couldn't hear it. Solitude made the noise unbearable for Clay, but so did its opposite. In Queens, crowds formed and panic metastasized. People ran. People wept. The police barely bothered to pretend to do anything.

Then: Clay found the way. It was like the previous forty-four minutes had never happened. He turned right and saw the sign promising eggs. It was too ridiculous to think about. Clay had no information, no cold Coke. Minutes before, he had decided that when he got back to the house, he'd bundle his family into the car and leave this place. He'd never wanted to see the house again.

Now the painted brick greeted him as an old friend. He cried from relief instead of fear. He turned off the car. He looked at the sky. He looked at the car. He looked toward the trees. As he ran toward the house, he began to recount what he knew.

The seas were said to be rising. People had been talking about Greenland a lot. Hurricane season was particularly bad. The forty-fifth president of the United States seemed to have dementia. Angela Merkel seemed to have Parkinson's disease. Ebola was back. There was something happening with interest rates. It was the second week of August. Classes would begin soon enough that you could measure the distance in days. His editor at the *New York Times Book Review* had probably emailed back with her comments on his review.

If the noise returned, say tonight, once the sun had set—once the profound dark of the farmland all around them asserted itself—he wouldn't survive it. You couldn't. That was the nature of the noise; it was horror, in some distilled way, in a single, very brief moment. He was rough with gooseflesh just revisiting it, trying to remember what it had sounded like as a means of deducing what it had been. He feared even going to sleep. How was he supposed to drive away?

Clay thought of his father. It seemed all too possible that his father, at home watching television in Minneapolis, knew nothing of a cryptic noise over Long Island. Something had to be truly big to affect life. When he was a teenager, his mother had suffered from what she assumed was the flu, a sleepiness she couldn't shake. She was dead of leukemia a few months after. Fifteen-year-old Clay had learned to cook Hamburger Helper and separate the white laundry from the colored laundry. People dropped dead, but you still needed to eat dinner. Maybe a war had begun, maybe there'd been some kind of industrial accident, maybe thousands of New Yorkers were trapped belowground in subway cars, maybe a missile had been fired, maybe some thing they'd never conceived of being possible was unfolding—all this was more or less true, as it happened—but Clay still felt like smoking a cigarette, or worried about the children's manners, and thought about what they would eat for dinner. Business as usual, the business of being alive.

Amanda, G. H., and Ruth were inside. They looked at him like people in a play, like they'd rehearsed this moment—you stand here, you stand here, you stand here, you come in. He felt like he should wait for applause, then wait for that to die down before he spoke. What was his line, anyway?

"Jesus Christ." Amanda did not race to hug him, did not shout it, it only fell out of her, a thud of relief.

"I'm back." Clay shrugged his shoulders. "Is everyone okay?"

G. H. looked vindicated. He looked pleased.

Amanda embraced him. She didn't say anything. She pulled away and looked up at him, then embraced him once more.

He didn't know what else to say. He'd heard the noise and winced and then the noise had abated and he could hear the blood thrumming through his body. "I'm okay. I'm here. Are you okay? Where are the kids?"

"We're okay," G. H. asserted. "Everyone is here. Everyone is okay."

"Maybe you'd like to join us." Ruth pushed the wine bottle in his direction like a bartender in a movie. She was more relieved than she had thought she would be. She realized it with shame, and then a sense of horror: she hadn't actually expected Clay to come back.

Clay scraped the chair's feet on the wood floor and sat. "Did you hear that?"

"Did you go into town? What happened?" Amanda held her husband's hand.

Clay couldn't reckon with that noise; he had to reckon with his own shame. He didn't know if he could admit it. "I didn't." He just said it, flat, no intonation.

"You didn't?" Amanda was confused, but they were all confused. "Where have you been?" She was angry.

Clay grew red. "I didn't get very far. And then I heard that noise—"

"But what were you doing?" Amanda was confused. "We've been waiting for you, I was going crazy—"

"I don't know. I had a cigarette. I was just gathering my thoughts. I had another. I started to drive, and then I heard that noise, and I came right back." He was lying because he was ashamed.

192 · RUMAAN ALAM

Amanda laughed. It came out cruel. "I thought you were dead out there!"

"So you didn't see anyone. Or anything that might help us figure out what's happening." G. H. wanted to keep them focused.

"You're here. Let's go. Let's get out of here. Let's go home!" Amanda wasn't sure if she meant it, or if she wanted to be persuaded otherwise, or what.

Clay shook his head. It was a lie. He had seen that woman. She'd been weeping. Had she found someone to help her? He couldn't bear admitting what sort of man he was when tested. It was easy enough to tell himself that that woman didn't matter. He could barely remember what she looked like. He wondered what she'd done when she heard the noise. "I didn't see anything or anyone. No cars, nothing."

"That's what it's like out here." G. H. tried to be rational. "That's why we like it out here. You often see no one."

They were all quiet.

Ruth was looking out the window, toward the pool. "It's dark out. It was just so clear." She stood. "Storm. Maybe that was thunder."

"That was not thunder." The sky was now, it was true, fat with clouds, gray fading to black. But Clay knew that much.

Ruth turned to look at them. "Years ago, G. H. took me to the ballet. *Swan Lake*."

The kind of thing Clay claimed was the reason to live in New York to begin with. But it was a logistical nightmare. Tickets for a mutually agreeable night, a place to have dinner at 6:30, eighteen dollars an hour for the sitter. They were too *busy*, committed to the notion of their own overcommitment. Could they not spare a few hours for transcendence?

"I remember thinking at first, oh, this is so odd. People in spangled costumes. They'd dance for a few minutes, then scurry off the stage, and then they'd do it again. I thought it was a story, but a ballet is just a bunch of short things loosely organized around a theme that doesn't make much sense to begin with."

Like life, Clay didn't say.

She went on. "Birds in white and birds in black, big sweeping music. I got interested. I think it was the most beautiful music I've ever heard in my life. There was this one dance I'd never heard before, and I don't know why they don't use it in movies and commercials, it's so beautiful. I bought the CDs. *Swan Lake*, conducted by André Previn. I remember the name of the piece. 'Pas d'Action,' 'Odette and the Prince.' " You never heard anything more—sweeping and romantic and then so sweet and alive."

"Probably." Amanda had no idea about ballet. She was happy the woman was talking, filling the silence.

"Tchaikovsky was thirty-five when he composed *Swan Lake*, did you know that? It was considered a failure, but you know—it's the very idea of ballet: a dancer dressed as a bird." She hesitated. "I remember thinking—well, it's a maudlin thought, but I suppose we all have thoughts like this from time to time—if I had to die, and we all do, if I could hear music, as I was dying, or have a piece of music that I knew would be the last thing I heard before I died, or that came to my mind as I was dying, even just the memory of it, I would want it to be that. Tchaikovsky, this dance from *Swan Lake*. That's what I'm sitting here thinking about. Though perhaps you won't like to hear it, but I was thinking, goddamn, I have those CDs in my apartment."

"You're not going to die out here, Ruth." Here? In this charming little house? Impossible. "We're safe here," Clay said. It was like that childhood game of telephone. They were talking amongst themselves and had lost track of things.

"How do you know?" She was calm. "The fact, the unfortunate fact, is that you don't know that. We don't know what is going to happen. I may never hear 'Pas d'Action,' 'Odette and the Prince,' ever again. I think

I have it." She tapped a temple. "I think I can hear it. The harp. The strings. But I might be wrong. What I have in here is beautiful, though."

"We're not on Mars. There are people just a few miles away. We'll hear something. We heard something. Maybe we'll hear it again." This was G. H., trying to be reassuring and rational at the same time. "We'll drive out to the neighbors. Or someone will come by. It's just a matter of time."

"I never want to hear that thing again." Clay wished he could have denied hearing the noise altogether. He wished he could imagine doing what G. H. described, but he couldn't. He was scared. He didn't want to leave, not because it wasn't prudent but because he was too afraid.

Amanda pulled away from her husband, who still had his arms on her, dazed relief, and looked at G. H. "You know, you look a little like Denzel Washington."

G. H. wasn't sure how to respond, and also it was not the first time he'd heard this.

"Has anyone ever told you that? And your last name is Washington! Any relation?" Amanda looked at her husband. "His name is *George Washington*. I don't know—I'm sorry, I know it's rude." She laughed, and none of them said anything.

25

From the other rooms, the children could not hear their mother's laughter. From the other rooms, the children had not heard their father's return. The little house was so well made (walls so solid!) and so seductive too that it made you forget other people altogether.

Archie ran the shower very hot. His balls were tight against his body, bumpy like he'd just got out of the pool. The muscles in his back softened as he watched the water twist down the drain, dirty and then clear. He dried his body on white towels. He put on boxer shorts and took to bed, where, unable to watch *The Office*, he diverted himself with that important repository, the hidden album on his phone. The pictures were mostly beautiful. The stuff Archie liked best was not so terrible. He was weirded out by the internet's complex configurations: three women, five women, seven women, massive dicks (his dick would never get so big, he worried), two men, three men, pretended incest, racial violence, spit, ropes, athletic equipment, public spectacle, stage lights, mussed makeup, swimming pools, toys and tools he didn't know the name of, the supposed beauty of punishment. He just liked women. Dark hair and tan skin. He preferred them to be completely naked, rather than posed with clothes to emphasize the parts of their body there for you to see: wooly sweater raised over heavy breasts with satin nipples, plaid skirt up over pale hips to show off what he called pussy because he was sure he didn't know the exact word for it, denim shorts slashed or torn, lips protruding. He liked her to look pretty and happy. Archie wanted to please and be pleased.

Rose pulled the down comforter of her parents' bed up to her chin, then over it, up to her nose, drawing in the smell of detergent and bath soap and her own skin and the lingering traces of her parents' chemical signature. This was comforting, almost canine. Her book was not an escape (adolescence's trials, the body's betrayals, the heart's new desires) but preparation, the Fodor's to a country she planned on visiting soon. But it couldn't hold her attention. She thought about the

198 · RUMAAN ALAM

quiet of the woods, punctured by that bang overhead. She could barely picture her little bedroom in Brooklyn. She shook her head to clear it, but that didn't do anything.

She didn't want to hide in bed. Rose didn't want to hide at all. She stood up and stretched as you might after a restorative night's sleep. She stretched her arms and legs, and they both felt powerful and alive. Rose walked to the window and tried to see into the trees. She wasn't sure what she was looking for, but she would know it when it appeared, and knew, too, that it would appear. Earlier, she'd wanted to prove that she'd seen those deer, but the ground had showed no sign of them. The beasts trod lightly on this earth.

She was standing before the glass back door, looking out at the flat sky, clouds close enough to touch. She saw that there was a crack in the pane and understood this had not been there before. It made sense. The rain was as it always was: hesitant at first, then confident. The trees were so thick with leaves, they'd sop up most of the water before it touched the ground. The overflow from the gutter over the door made a kind of waterfall. What did the deer do when it rained? Did animals care about getting wet? Rose wished she could go for another swim, or just sit in the hot tub. She wished for a little more vacation, even just an hour.

The phone in one hand and himself in the other, Archie's body did not respond as it usually did. He could come in the morning's shower and in his night-time bedroom lit by the laptop, volume turned low. Sometimes afternoons too: huddled in the drafty pee-smelling cubicle, spit on palm. First ropes of cum, then an abbreviated sneeze of the stuff, finally a dry shudder, his dick red and tired and maybe a little sore. He'd always swear it off but—it finds a way. It was life!

There was a storm forming outside, and the light was strange, but even if not for that, Archie would have had no idea how to guess what time it was. He knew it was odd that the people who owned the house had shown up, but he didn't care, or they seemed nice. Mr. Washington had asked him the kinds of questions that grown-ups always asked, and had seemed nice. Archie abandoned his phone. He slipped into the beautiful void. If he dreamed of anything (the noise?), it was with some part of his mind so distant he barely controlled it.

Did he feel warm? Well, he'd just taken a shower. When he tucked his wrist under his cheek, that told him nothing; touching your own skin is not diagnostic. The body was a splendid and complicated machine, almost always humming along happily. When something went wrong, the body was smart enough to make accommodations. The light was muddled and soupy, the room filled with the music of rain on the roof overhead and the unassuming sound of objects in space— the presence of Archie's body, his bed, his pillows, his glass of water, his paperback of *Nine Stories*, the wet towel curled on the floor like a napping pet. It was like the white-noise machine his parents had used to trick the infant him to sleep.

Washing her hands, Ruth could not hear the rain. Then she left the guest bath and saw the tumble of water and understood. The wine had done nothing to her. She was not sleepy, or pacified, or distracted. She gathered their dirty clothes into a little pile. How were there so many already? There was something comforting about the yellow of the bedside lamps and the gray outside the windows. She could have got into that bed and read a book. She might even have dozed in that indolent way you do when you're in a vacation home— not for need of rest but because you can.

Instead, she went to the walk-in closet down the hallway, found a laundry basket on the shelf beside all of George's provisions, those bottles of wine, those helpful tins, those sturdy plastic containers of thousands and thousands of calories. She allowed herself to think—*good*. They were prepared for whatever this was. She'd have thought this might comfort her, but she didn't want cans of tomatoes or sticky Kind bars. It was fruitless to dwell on what it was she wanted, which perhaps explained her resolve to simply *do* something. Ruth filled the basket with their dirty laundry. She righted the throw pillows on the bed. She put the useless television remote control back onto the dresser. She turned off the reading lamps that no one was using. She retrieved the damp towels from the bathroom.

It was too intimate, but she knew she should invite Amanda to put in her dirty clothes. It would be a more efficient use of power and water. It would be neighborly, though that word didn't describe their relationship—maybe no word could. Ruth knew a conversation was warranted, and knew that it would demand that she pretend to be a better person than she felt like being. She thought of the satisfying weight of her grandsons on her body.

Rose put her hand on the window. It was cold, as glass tended to be. There was something satisfying about the surface of the swimming pool, roiled and rippled by the steady rain. There was no thunder, and anyway, Rose understood that the noise before had not been thunder. She saw the temptation in believing that, but she knew in her own teenage way that belief and fact had nothing to do with each other.

The question was not what that had been; the question was what they would do next. Rose knew that her parents did not take her seriously, did not think her grown. But Rose knew that their troubles were not a matter of some sound overhead. She'd seen what the problem was, and she'd try to solve it. Then she remembered that her mother had promised her that when it rained, they would bake a cake, so Rose forgot her book and went to do just that.

26

Television would have been palliative. Television would have stunned them, entertained them, informed them or helped them forget. Instead: the three of them sitting around a television that showed them nothing, the pleasant orchestra of the rain against skylight, roof, deck, canvas umbrella, treetop, and the clatter of Rose—"I can do it by myself!"—in the kitchen, and then the chemical scent of her cake from a box, puffing up in the gas oven.

"We need to fill the bathtubs." Amanda wasn't sure what was required. She was guessing.

"Fill the bathtubs?" Clay took it for a figure of speech.

She lowered her voice. "In case—the water."

"Does the water not run if the power goes out?" Clay had no idea.

It did not. The next day, or the day after that, certainly the day following that one, some residents of the uppermost apartments in Manhattan would fall into the delirium that presaged their eventual dehydration. "I think that's right. An electric pump fills the reservoir. So if the power goes, the water does too." G. H. marveled that their power still held on. He credited the well-made little house, even though he knew that had nothing to do with it.

"Do you think the power is going to go out?" Clay thought the day—the smell of yellow sponge, the percussion of the rain—seemed almost unnervingly normal.

"It goes out in storms, doesn't it? Like, downed branches? And if there's something wrong in the city. And then that noise, whatever that was? I think we're lucky that it's still on, but maybe we shouldn't push our luck." Amanda looked at her husband. "Go!"

Clay got up and went to do as entreated, without mentioning the fact that they weren't his tubs and it wasn't his water.

Amanda leaned forward in her seat, toward G. H. across from her. "There's no thunder. No lightning, even. Just rain."

"I didn't really think it was thunder anyway."

"So what was it?" She was whispering because she did not want Rose to hear. She did not think the girl stupid, she just thought she might protect her.

"I wish I knew."

"What are we doing?"

"I'm waiting for the cake your daughter is baking."

"Should we leave?" She looked at the older man like he was the father she had never had, the one she could trust for sound advice. "Wouldn't we be better— safer—at home, in the city, around other people?"

"I don't know."

"I would feel better if I just knew what was happening." Amanda looked toward the hall, could hear the plash of water in the bathtub. These words were not true, but she did not know that.

Clay returned, wiping hands on shorts. "That's done."

"There's a tub downstairs. I'll do the same." G. H. nodded his thanks.

"So there's that." Amanda was trying to convince herself. "We have some water. And we don't even need it. Maybe we won't at all."

"Better to be prepared," Clay agreed.

"Do you think we should go home?" Amanda looked at her husband.

"Or we can just go back to town tomorrow? Or go for the first time," G. H. corrected himself.

"I'm sorry." Clay put his hands on his knees. The gesture was sheepish.

"What?" Amanda asked.

"I should have— I heard the noise and I came back, I was worried. But! I didn't see any cars." Clay did not tell them about the woman. He wondered if she was out in the rain.

"I thought you were— I didn't know what had happened to you."

G. H. was understanding. "You see no cars a lot of the time. It depends on the time of year, I guess. But it's quiet. That's why we moved here in the first place."

"I think we should just sit tight." Clay didn't want to go back onto those confounding roads.

"How can you say that?" Amanda asked. Parenthood required pretending bravado, derring-do, courage, conviction. It was just instinct, it was just love.

"It's pouring. Maybe it's not the best idea to trek out in a storm."

"Fine. But tomorrow." Amanda was prompting him.

"We'll go to town," Clay said. "Then we can— decide. If the power is out in the city maybe we should wait things out."

"Here?" They did have the lease. That didn't seem

to matter as much. Amanda would prepare to demonstrate her faith. She'd pack up their things, be ready to leave. It was a statement of purpose.

"Tomorrow. Clay, you and me, we'll go in the morning. I know the way." G. H. didn't believe Clay's story, and he was right not to. "Then we'll see where we are after that. If there's power, if there's a problem, what that noise was. We'll know more, and once we know more, we can decide the best thing to do." He looked up at the girl approaching the adults. G. H. felt the same urge Amanda had. "It smells delicious in here." He said it jauntily but meant it sincerely.

"It just needs to cool before I frost it."

"It's done already?" Amanda tried to determine the time. "We should save it for after dinner."

"I made layers, so it bakes faster. Two little cakes instead of one big one. I wish I had things to decorate it. Sprinkles and stuff."

"You might want to look in the pantry. Go ask Mrs. Washington to show you where she keeps all the baking things. I wouldn't be surprised if we had some supplies on hand." The girl was nothing like his daughter, but naturally that was who he thought of.

"I should get something together for dinner." Clay thought it atonement for his earlier failure. He'd filled the tubs, he'd feed them dinner, he'd prove his value.

"Rose, before you get into the cake decorating, let's tidy up the kitchen."

"Where's Archie?" Amanda wanted the children out of sight but could not get them out of mind.

Clay shrugged. "Maybe he's napping."

"I should get him up." There was that danger, she knew, in napping too late—the grogginess nothing would dispel. As a toddler, he'd wake with his face creased from the bedding, red from the exertion of rest, grumpy and unable to do more than pout for at least ten minutes. She offered G. H. an "Excuse me," then went to the boy's door. Amanda knocked, because teenagers needed the respect of that first (she'd seen some things), then pushed the door open, saying his name.

The boy did not stir, did not seem to register her presence.

"Archie?" She could see his shape, twisted in the blankets. "Honey, are you sleeping?"

He said nothing, if he heard her, so Amanda pulled the covers from his face, revealing his hair, in glorious disarray, tendrils this way and that like the roots of an old tree. She smoothed his locks, a palm on his forehead by reflex. Was he warm from fever or warm from slumber? "Archie?"

He opened his eyes, not blinking; asleep and then

not. He looked at his mother, but she did not come into focus.

"Archie? Are you feeling okay?"

He exhaled slowly, a long and tremulous breath. He did not know where he was, he did not understand what was happening. He sat up, this movement abrupt too. He opened his mouth, not to speak, but to move his jaw, which hurt, or of which he was aware, in some way that seemed new or different or wrong. "I don't know."

"What do you mean, you don't know?" She pulled the duvet back, revealing his thin frame, releasing the radiant heat of his body, so powerful she could feel it without laying hands on him. "Archie?"

He made a sound, like a hum. He leaned forward and vomited onto his own lap.

27

Parenthood hardened you. Your task was upkeep of the body, and you understood what that entailed. The sight of vomit once made her retch, but her children's—Amanda faced it. Crisis made her rational. She called to Clay. She washed her son's body just as she had when he'd been a boy.

When they were babies, Clay and Amanda played man-on-man defense. That first wretched winter, Clay would take Archie to the New York City Transit Museum, an indoor attraction but always very cold, since it was built in an old subway station. Amanda would pace the apartment with Rosie, desperate for the tit, listening to the album Björk had made about how great it was to have sex with Matthew Barney. If she thought about it, Amanda could still hear the creak of floor-board underfoot in that one spot near the kitchen. If he thought about it, Clay could still picture the trains from a more innocent era—rattan seats, ceiling fans—parked on the museum's obsolete tracks. Amanda stripped the soiled bedding. Clay took the boy to the living room.

"We have a thermometer." Ruth, prudent, had stocked the bathroom. Analgesics for adults and children, bandages, iodine, saline, petroleum jelly.

"That would be great." Clay helped the boy into his too-big sweatshirt; he smoothed his mussed hair. He sat beside him on the sofa, and they looked toward the back of the house, at the drama of the rain filling the swimming pool.

Maternal muscle memory was strong. Ruth returned with supplies. "Let's take his temperature."

So, too, was paternal instinct. G. H. helped Rose find the hidden stores: icing sugar, tubes of decorative gels, birthday candles, sprinkles rattling in plastic jars. Rose was not a fool, but happy enough to be diverted. They coaxed the cake onto a plate, and she spun it expertly beneath the spatula, stationary, thick with frosting.

"Thank you," Clay said.

Ruth held the boy's chin, placed the point of the glass tube beneath his tongue. "You do feel warm. But let's just see how warm."

"How do you feel now, bud?" Clay relied on these masculine affections when he was most worried. He'd already asked. Archie had already answered. He wanted to put an arm around him, wanted to fold him into his body, but the boy wouldn't like that because the boy was nearly a man.

"I'm fine." Archie mumbled through the thermometer, unable to achieve his characteristic adolescent disdain.

Ruth studied the inscrutable instrument. "One hundred and two. Not so bad. Not so good."

"Drink your water, pal." Clay pressed the glass into the boy's hand.

"Take these." Ruth shook out two Tylenol just as G. H. and Rose were peppering the cake with sugar confetti, a nice little duet.

Archie did as he was bid. He held a sip of the liquid in his mouth, then put the pills into that. He swallowed and tried to tell if his throat was tender. He wanted to watch television, or go back to his house, or lose himself in his phone, but none of these were possible, so he just sat there, saying nothing.

"I'm going to go help Amanda." Ruth was pleased

to have a problem to solve, or a problem that she might solve. "You just rest here."

Finding the bathtub full of the water that was meant to save their lives, Amanda took the soiled sheets to the master bathroom, rinsed the (mercifully watery) vomit in the tiled shower. She squeezed them as dry as she could, twisting the cotton until she feared it would rend. She was angry, and this was something to do with that feeling. She dried her hands and went into the bedroom. How quickly they spread out: a tangle of dirty underwear, used paper napkin, magazine, glass of water, all these little signs that they existed and endured. Trees marked their lives in rings that can't be seen; people, in the garbage they left everywhere, a way of insisting on their own importance. Amanda began righting the room.

"Knock knock." Ruth said it like a character in a television show as she strode down the hall and into the room, laundry basket at her hip. "I don't mean to interrupt. I thought I might do the wash anyway, though."

Amanda performed a kind of curtsy for some reason. Well, it was the woman's room. "I'm sorry. I can do Archie's sheets."

"Don't be sorry. Just throw them in here. He seems fine. A temperature. One hundred and two."

"One hundred and two?"

"It sounds high, but you know they are high when they're kids. Those showroom-new immune systems working overtime. I gave him some Tylenol."

"Thank you."

"You can put your clothes in too. I just—while the power is still on."

It was too intimate, but Ruth had foresight. It would save them the trek to the Laundromat when they got home. Amanda did not know that the Laundromat was closed. She did not know that the Chinese man who ran it was inside the elevator that carried passengers between the turnstiles and the platform at the R train station in Brooklyn Heights, and he'd been there for hours, and he'd die there, though that was many hours in the future yet. "That's smart. Thank you."

They considered each other like they were meant to duel. Maybe that was inevitable. Ruth pitied the woman. She knew what was required of her, and hated it. She had to pretend her way to being a good person. But what about Maya and the boys? "You know, you could stay. If you wanted."

The little house as life raft. Ignorance as a kind of knowing. This did not seduce Amanda. An eternity (as though that were granted) with these people. Part of her still wondered whether this wasn't a con or a delusion. It was torture, a home invasion without rape or guns. Still, this woman was the nearest an ally Amanda had. She shook her head. "Archie needs a doctor."

"What if we all do? What if it's inside us? What if something is beginning, or everything is ending?" This subtext was inescapable. People kept calling the Amazon the planet's lungs. Waist-deep water was lapping against Venetian marble, and tourists were smiling and taking snapshots. It was like some tacit agreement; everyone had ceded to things just falling apart. That it was common knowledge that things were bad surely meant they were actually worse. Ruth wasn't this kind of person, but she could feel disease blooming inside her body. It was everywhere, inescapable.

"I can't think about what we don't know. I need to focus on this. Archie needs a doctor, I'll take him to a doctor tomorrow morning."

"But you're afraid. I'm afraid."

"That's not getting us anywhere. I can't stay here. I can't hide. I'm his mother. What else can we do?"

Ruth sat on the bed's edge. She couldn't go to town or beyond, to Northampton. She wanted to just lie in her bed. "I guess you're right."

"Say something to make me feel better." Amanda was searching for friendship or humanity or reassurance or relief.

Ruth crossed her legs and looked up at her. "I can't do that. Comforting."

Amanda was immediately disappointed.

"Maybe I need it. Comforting." She was eager to wash the clothes. The neutral smell of the soap, the thunder of the water. "So I can't provide it. But stay. I think you should. I think it makes sense. Even if I can't make you feel better. I can't say something wise and churchy for you."

"I know—I know you can't."

"At least you have your children here with you. I don't know what's happening to my daughter. I don't know what's happening to my grandsons. We don't know anything about the world. That is what it is."

Amanda knew this was the way it had always been. She couldn't help but wish it were otherwise. Her clothes smelled of her son's vomit, and the air smelled of her daughter's cake. "Let's eat something. I'm going to take a shower, and then we should eat something. I think that will help." No, that wasn't quite it. "I can't think of anything else to do."

28

There was almost something festive about it. A drink before the war. Seen one way, it was placid, it was inviting, it was a vacation. Enterprising Ruth had produced a can of chicken soup, which Archie reluctantly spooned. Amanda tucked him into his remade bed. Enterprising Rose remembered: she had downloaded a movie to her mother's laptop a year earlier. She wasn't that interested in it, but it was better than nothing. Amanda sent her to bed with a slice of cake and the almost-obsolete computer, and the four adults had an adult evening, or the candor they couldn't enjoy when little ears were listening. G. H. paged through an old *Economist*. Ruth filled porcelain bowls with baby carrots and hummus. Amanda nursed a glass of wine. Clay stood at the island, improvising a sausage pasta.

The rain had abated, the deck dry beneath the eaves. But they'd dine inside, not for fear of the mosquitoes in their end-of-season death throes. The woods menaced them. The moon was waxing, pale yellow, proud through the broken clouds. There was no aftershock to the noise, or there was, and it was all in their heads. Maybe what they'd heard was the sky itself cracking, like Henny Penny foretold. It seemed likely as anything. No one knew what was happening to them, and maybe because of that the rite was strangely joyous, or maybe it was collective hysteria, or maybe it was the chardonnay, cold and the color of apple juice.

It felt practiced or familiar as Thanksgiving, the passing of food on plates, the filling of glasses, the chit-chat. Did anyone want to hear George's stories? A client bilked out of a fortune when a Basquiat was revealed a forgery, the man who'd shifted hundreds of thousands of dollars to his seven-month-old to sidestep a prenup, the man who'd lost three million in Macau, the client who needed cash to pay one of the New York Yankees to bless his son's bar mitzvah. His stories were about money, not men; money awe-inspiring and irrational and almost all-powerful. George thought money could explain what was happening to them, and that time would tell if money would save them from it. If these people did leave the next day, he'd have to remember to give them a thousand dollars for their trouble. G. H. wasn't sure if he thought they would leave, though.

Dessert, why not? There was an air of finality, at least for Clay. The now-clean clothes tumbled about in the hot embrace of the four-thousand-dollar dryer. He thought Archie's fever would break, thought he'd ask G. H. for directions, a pencil sketch, safe deliverance. He thought the morning would come and surprise them with its beauty and they'd drive home.

They sliced Rose's cake. Ruth put cardboard pints of ice cream onto the table. The well-stocked kitchen had two stainless steel ice cream scoops. There were enough dishes to fill the washer.

Amanda said it: "Well, the electricity is still on." You stopped noticing a thing like the flow of power, a thing you couldn't see but derived some comfort from, rather like God. The water was slowly, very slowly, draining from the tub in the children's bath, but she didn't know that.

The conversation turned to places they'd traveled. G. H., sardonic, said, "You must have had more enjoyable vacations than this one."

Amanda thought of those places where nights never grew dark: Helsinki, St. Petersburg, small towns in Alaska built for men paid to do things to the earth. She feared the return of that noise, unfathomable in the dark. They already knew nothing. "Disney?" She laughed. She'd hated it at the time but cherished the memory.

"Archie threw up then too," Clay said. He wanted to think of it like that—that vacation meant kids naturally capitulated to virus. Archie, always with the throwing up! Archie, cut it out! This was more enjoyable than believing Archie ill.

Ruth talked about Paris. She and Maya had teatime at the George V, tried on shoes at the Galeries Lafayette, rode the carousel in the Tuileries, though at thirteen Maya considered it beneath her. "A city as gorgeous as you've always been told it is."

"We should do that for winter break. Paris is so beautiful you don't even care if it's cold." Clay saw his kids on the deck of the Eiffel Tower, puffs of frosty breath as they surveyed the world at their feet. He remembered footage of Paris flooding—when was that? The Louvre had moved thirty-five thousand works of art so the Seine wouldn't destroy them. "We'll see *The Lady and the Unicorn.*"

"Sounds expensive." Idle promises scared Amanda. What if it was a war, big enough to ensnare the entire world, and national borders became like castle walls? She didn't know that it was worse, that war could not describe it. Those planes had been sent from Rome,

New York, to meet another, approaching from western Africa. Bad intelligence: they ended up killing four hundred odd souls before they got near enough our borders to have to fill out their immigration paperwork. The pace of things used to be slower. Now a nut didn't have to shoot an archduke; every day was a jumble of near-simultaneous oddity.

The cardboard cartons emptied. Everyone admired the cake made from a box. Smudges of chocolate hardened on plates. When the true dark set in, the night's winged creatures would beat softly against the glass, the outside lights would click on, illuminating the boughs overhead. A silence settled, one of those natural intervals sometimes experienced in restaurants or at parties when talk relaxes and the assembled company lean forward, straining as though to hear something barely discernible. There were no eggs left in the refrigerator, but perhaps they could serve cereal for breakfast.

They decided, without discussing, to simply sit and feel satisfied. G. H. fiddled with his glass. Clay twitched with that delirious urge to smoke a cigarette, so powerful it was a little frightening. He had to confront the fact that he was weak. Ruth looked toward the window and saw mostly her own reflection. Amanda retrieved the bottle of vodka she'd bought the day they arrived.

222 • RUMAAN ALAM

G. H. sliced lemons into rounds, yellow coins, fat with flavor.

When Amanda got to the bottom of the first drink, she dug her fingers through the ice and set the citrus on her tongue like the Catholics did with the body of Christ. Transubstantiated into someone new. She was drunk. The tell was the volume of her voice. "I'll have another." This was a command more than a request.

G. H. poured. "My pleasure."

Clay smelled of the cigarette he'd just returned from enjoying, though enjoyment wasn't much a part of it. The crickets conspiring. The possibility of something out there. He'd hoped to see headlights, maybe a plane crossing the sky. There were studies about solitary confinement making you mad. He missed the presence of other humans, and he was putting on a brave front because that was his job as a man. "George, will you make us a map? Tomorrow? You'll show us the way. Clearly I can't be trusted."

"I'll drive into town. You can follow me."

Ruth did not say anything.

Amanda was afraid of slurring and seeming more drunk than she knew she was. She was a woman in control of things. "Are you going to come back . . . here?"

"Yes, we are." Ruth would go with him. She wouldn't

stay there alone. She wanted them to leave and to stay. She could not be indifferent, even though she wanted to be. She did not want to feel guilt.

"I wish I knew the roads to Northampton." G. H. was reserved. "It's far. We'll just hope that the phones . . ." He didn't bother concluding.

"We need to take care of Archie—" Amanda's falter said what needed to be said. The boy was sick. It didn't matter what caused it, only what they did about it. All those years fretting about the expensive epinephrine autoinjector, at the boy's side like the president and the nuclear codes, and Archie was undone by a noise. Parenthood was never knowing what was going to hurt your kids, but knowing only that something, inevitably, would.

"Before you go, I'll give you your cash back." G. H. was fair, or a deal was a deal. He was drinking the vodka too. The four of them were united in their search for the temporary peace of oblivion. It almost worked; he almost forgot why they were together in the first place.

"I'm not going to forget that, I can assure you." Clay tried to make a joke of it. Maybe they needed that money to pay the medical bills. Maybe they needed that money to replace a refrigerator full of rotting food. Maybe his editor at the *New York Times Book Review* would so love his essay she'd offer him a contract. Anything, anything, was possible. He put a hand on his wife's to tell her that he thought they were making the right choice.

"We're all going to be fine." Amanda was not addressing him alone, drunk enough not to care that these people were involved. They were family now, or something.

"If it's your last night of vacation, you should enjoy it." Ruth stacked soiled plates one atop the other, leaving aside the fact that she enjoyed restoring order. These people had become their friends, their guests, and Ruth the host, and she just needed to clear the table.

"To enjoyment. To the enjoyment of vacations. To the enjoyment of any moment in life, I guess. Enjoying a moment is a victory. I think we need to hold on to those." G. H. raised his glass. The gesture was sincere.

"I'll enjoy, I'll enjoy." Amanda felt defensive. Like saying: I am having a good time, I am a good time. Optimists believed they could change the world. They thought if you looked on the bright side, the less bright side would no longer exist.

"It's not an order, it's an invitation." G. H. felt at ease. He couldn't wait to see the markets. He couldn't wait to figure out who had got rich, because in such moments, someone brave or just lucky always did. He hoped the night would grow cold. He wanted to stand outside and shiver, then sink into the hot tub and look at the black limbs of the trees.

Amanda refilled her drink. She wanted more ice cream, the lavish sweetness in her mouth. There was no more, but there were doughnuts, there was a package of cookies, she had options. She knew before they went to bed that night she'd steal into the kitchen, tear through whatever she found, palms full of salty Goldfish crackers, limp American cheese, a finger in the hummus. As she stood, the room moved, a little. The table under her fingertips steadied her.

"I think I'll have another." Ruth closed the dishwasher door, satisfied.

"I should fold the laundry. Maybe pack us up." Amanda stood.

"I can help you. Fold. We can fold. Pack—let's go one step at a time."

"I think we should be prepared," Amanda said.

"Perhaps we'll have a nightcap later?" Clay felt it was good manners. Maybe this was their last night together. It seemed they'd been together for weeks. It had been one day.

In the bedroom, they worked in silence. The clothes, still warm, were sorted into tidy piles, dropped to the

226 · RUMAAN ALAM

bottom of the rolling duffel. "I have to remember to go outside and get everyone's flip-flops."

"Let's just be cautious."

"I'm packing. We're not coming back here. We're going home."

Clay understood her insistence. If they thought it, it would be so. He took clean underpants from the chest of drawers and placed them atop the bed. "It's been a strange day. I need reality."

Amanda sat on the bed. "A day that felt like a week."

"Could it be that we're addicted to our phones? Like an actual addiction? Because I feel unwell." Clay was charging his, wanted to be sure it was ready when the network came back online.

Amanda fretted. "What if that noise made us sick?"

"It might be possible." What if the hair fell from his head, as it did for chemotherapy patients on television shows, what if his rubbery fingernails peeled back to reveal the softest part of the body, what if his bones hollowed and weakened, what if his blood ran with poison, what if tumors lurked in the space behind his eyeballs, grew slowly as Amanda's lungs had filled that inflatable pool toy, one breath, then the next, until the thing was a softball pressing into his eye socket?

"And those people." She whispered this. She was betraying them. She hated George Washington (what sort of name was that?) and she hated Ruth and she blamed them for bringing the world into this house. Amanda wanted to be safely buckled into the front seat, her left hand straying unconsciously to squeeze Clay's right arm, recumbent atop the gearshift. She wanted to drive away from this place and these people.

Fear was private. It was primal. It was something you guarded because you thought you could defuse it that way. How could they continue to love each other, having realized that they could not save each other? No one person could stop a determined terrorist or the gradual change in the oceans' pH. The world was lost, and there was nothing that Clay or Amanda could do about it, so why discuss?

In other words: The world was over, so why not dance? The morning would come, so why not sleep? An end was inevitable, so why not drink, eat, enjoy the moment, whatever it contained? "You know what I feel like doing?" Clay pulled his shirt over his head and tossed it to Amanda for the pile of dirty things, grinning and tumescent.

29

Maybe Amanda was greedy. Sometimes, not knowing what else to do, you had sex. Clay could make her feel better not psychically but physically. She let him carry her away from herself. In the body she was far from the mind. She opened herself to it, though maybe the vodka helped. She consented. More than. She wanted it. She pushed off her humid underwear. She lay back on the bright white duvet. The clothes she was packing up fell to the wood floor.

The shirt Clay wore remembered the sudden sweat, a fear response to that noise. She buried her nose in his armpit and closed her eyes. She traced the inside of his thigh and tasted salt. The sounds they made were close to screams. It didn't seem to matter, nothing did. She let them rise from somewhere deep in her chest, like she imagined opera singers did. The clap of flesh against flesh. Hair lacquered to skin with spit. The opportunity to forget.

Amanda thought of the best worst things, that's what sexual fantasy was. One dick, two dicks, three dicks, four! She thought of G. H. leering at her from the threshold, then coming into the room to offer some pointers, to encourage Clay in his fucking, to— sure why not—fuck her himself. Fuck, fuck, forget. She came once, twice. What was left on her stomach was enough to fill a shot glass, was the work of a younger man. It was enough to make a baby. You needed so little for that. They could make two, three, ten, an army of them, alternate versions of the children they already had, pink and clean and healthy and strong, a new world order because the old world was so out of order. Amanda propped herself up on her elbows. The stuff slid down her like a snail on a sedge, onto that beautiful white duvet.

Clay was out of breath. Fucking her like that was like inflating fifty pool floats. Sometimes he could picture a tumor blossoming in his lungs, black and terrible. Still, you couldn't live without risk. He lay on his stomach, then rolled onto his back. The sweat on his skin had its intended, cooling effect. "I love you." His voice emerged hoarse after all those exhalations and exhortations. He did not feel cowed by what they'd just done. He felt restored. He thought of Ruth and vowed that when they got back to their apartment, he would listen to *Swan Lake*. And he did love Amanda, he loved her, he *loved*. You endured as long as that was the case.

It felt insincere, to return a declaration of love. An echo was just a trick of physics. She felt free. "I'm worried about Archie."

It was maybe the best sex they'd had, though of course pleasure, like pain, was so soon forgotten. "He'll be okay. We'll get home, we'll see Dr. Wilcox."

She prodded at the stain on the bedspread, worried.

"Who cares about that?" He dipped a finger into his semen like a quill into ink. He wrote phantom letters on her belly.

She'd strip this bed, too, leave the linens on the floor of the laundry room. "Maybe when we're back we can do something special. It's still our vacation. We could drive out to Hoboken and check into a hotel with a rooftop pool. I bet that would be cheap."

"I want to stop at a diner on the way home." Clay was hungry right then. "One of those old-fashioned places. Chrome. Jukeboxes. Corned beef hash." The only things a person ever wanted were food and home.

"A staycation. The movies. Go to the Met. Dinner